T0207684

UNPLEASANT PASTURES

Charles Feggans

authorHOUSE®

AuthorHouse™
1663 Liberty Drive
Bloomington, IN 47403
www.authorhouse.com
Phone: 1 (800) 839-8640

Published by AuthorHouse 02/11/2020

ISBN: 978-1-7283-3588-9 (sc)
ISBN: 978-1-7283-3587-2 (e)

Contents

INTRODUCTION

The story takes place in Vietnam, 16 miles South of the Border separating North and South Vietnam territories in a place called Happy Valley right outside of DaNang.

The story gets up close and personal with the characters. You see each character as a real person. Some are funny and some are laid back. The story gives a one-sided picture of what a soldier sees and endures during his first day stationed in a war zone camp where the weather is unbearably hot with no relieve in sight and hostile forces at times make life during the night scary in their attempt to destroy the camp. The main two Marine characters are Jeff and Vick. Jeff is sent to Vick's outfit and Vick becomes his tour guide inside the camp and areas away from the camp. Together they bring the story to life.

CHAPTER ONE

Just above the thin layers of puffy white cotton clouds, the massive, metal structure of a lone commercial aircraft soared through the air. Now and then its body would shift slightly to the left or to the right as though it was thrown off balance by some invisible force, trying to redirect its chartered course. Blinding reflections of undying brilliant rays, produced by the sun, flickered along its long sleek outer shell.

The atmosphere surrounding the aircraft was filled with a continuous, twirling sound of turbine engines.

Throughout the confined areas within the aircraft, a string of overhead lights contributed to the pure light, pouring in through scattered, non-shaded portholes.

The whirling sound just beyond the outer shell of the aircraft became a whisper within its massive structure.

A sea of green clothed Marines occupied every available seat. Most of them slept while the remaining few found ways to arbitrarily occupy or amuse themselves.

About one-third of the way down into the seated area from the front row, just behind the right wing, Jeff Richards sat between two Marines. The three bodies posed lifelessly as they appeared to be sleeping sound. Slowly Jeff started to stir.

He opened his mouth extremely wide to ease the pressure building up within his head. Sudden chain reactions, of inner popping sensations, brought instant relief to his ears.

He tossed slightly before maneuvering his arms above his head in a long, twisting stretch. After receiving the thrill of being fully extended, he yawned and squinted before finally opening his eyes. The feeling of being out of place with his arms extended, made him place them on his lap.

The slight turning of the plane gave him cause to look out his side window. He sat momentarily staring at just pure sky and the heavens. The plane began to level off, slicing through piles of thin, scattered clouds.

Jeff was a black, fair-complexioned young man, just turning nineteen, and sporting a golden suntan, something he picked up during jungle training in California.

His short, neatly curled hair was within military regulations, something out of the ordinary for him. If his mother could see him now, she would marvel at how well the Marine Corp had groomed and developed him. Before joining up, his hair was kept long and his body was lanky with no definition, and now he was a picture of health.

He came from a well to do family. As an only child, Jeff never had to want for anything. He always had the best of everything, food, clothing, schooling and most of all, lots of gifts.

After graduating from Junior High School, and entering Senior High School, Jeff had grown to a point where he wanted to become his own man. He was tired of dressing, acting and being paraded around under his father's pressures.

Despite his parents objections, he joined the Marine Corps right after graduation to experience life from a less fortunate point of view. So here he was. His first plane trip without them, sitting among a sea of 264 green-clothed Marines, his newly founded family.

Soon, he and the others would be landing in Central Viet Nam after an all-night flight from California.

This time, the plane made a descending turn as it moved below the clouds, exposing winding waterways, surrounded by large plots of dense, green vegetation.

Jeff's eyes followed a winding waterway until a wide airstrip came into view, which seemed to revolve around the window.

He turned his head away just in time to catch a side glimpse of a well defined stewardess making her way to the rear of the plane, checking seatbelts and overhead compartments. Several Marines watched in delight, while others gathered loose articles belonging to them.

Both Marines on each of Jeff's flanks suddenly came back to life. One began looking around. "It's day light already?"

"Yep," Jeff voluntarily answered.

"Anybody know where we at?"

"Almost home, The Nam."

He went to relaxing in his seat. The other Marine sat quietly.

Jeff took a photograph from his pocket and stared at it. The picture was taken at his nineteenth birthday party, three months before going to California for jungle training. His father and girlfriend flanked him as he bent to extinguish the candles on his cake. Unfortunately, his mother had been away in another country, taking care of business during his entire leave, and therefore was not present.

His attire comprised of a new suit his father had purchased for this occasion. He would have preferred wearing his uniform, but his father had ill feelings about fighting a war he didn't understand. Just the same, Jeff felt good knowing he had earned his own Marine uniform, and felt proud wherever he displayed it. He smiled and casually replaced it in a pocket near his heart.

The aircraft had prepared to land. Jeff was staring toward the front when he heard the squealing sound of rubber brushing against the concrete runway. *Oh finally, I thought this plane would never land,* was the thought running through his mine. He loosened his seat belt.

The passengers began to mumble among themselves, and moved around during removal of their seatbelts.

"May I have your attention?" Came the Captain's voice over the intercom. "Present ground temperature for this July day is one hundred six degrees. Be prepared for a sudden blast of heat as you exit the plane. On behalf of the crew and myself, we wish you a safe tour of duty. Our prayers go with you, and we hope to see you again next year on your returning flight."

"This doesn't sound good at all," one Marine said, who was sitting by the window half dazed. "Do you think I can hide on this plane and go back to the States with the crew?"

Jeff was lost in his own little world. He didn't respond. He- couldn't imagine what this degree of heat felt like. His words turned to mutter as he talked softly, "I can't believe what he said about the temperature."

The Marine beside him realizing Jeff had nixed him off, started to give concern to Jeff's thought. "He's for real. I've been listening to the news back home, and he's not joking."

Still the daze lingered over him, "I can't image what it's going to be like around 2:30 pm, may be I'll just lay down and die."

"Some days are worse than this. We just jumped out of the frying pan and into the fire."

Jeff turned to face him. "That's hot for a morning. I

might become a heat casualty before I even get off this plane. I can't even imagine temperature being that hot."

The plane taxied to a stop on a barren section of the airport. Several stewardess took up positions throughout the cabin as the door opened. Marines filled the aisle, and the line slowly inched toward the front.

Jeff moved along with the others. The whistling engines died. A wave of heat struck him hard as he neared the exit. It began penetrating his uniform and exposed body parts. He had made up his mind that if the others could deal with it, he would do like wise. He exchanged a smile with the stewardess posted at the top step, and emerged into the bright sunlight and breathtaking heat. The heat quickly covered his body like a blanket.

How can anyone live under these conditions? He wondered. *This is insane.*

He walked down the steps, blowing into one hand to see if air existed in the smelting atmosphere. Convinced there was, but not satisfied, he moved out of line, stopped, shaded his eyes from the sun to look around before starting to follow the line to waiting buses.

The thought about the heat seemed silly. He dismisses it from his mind.

Realizing he was falling behind, he quickly hastened his pace.

He boarded and took a window seat near the middle of

the bus. The hot vinyl seat made him stir uncomfortably and perspiration began to stain his clothing. He glanced through the open window, taking a last minute survey of the area. To the far side of a remote runway, Jeff saw several men loading aluminum caskets from several piles into a cargo plane. *They must be frying the bodies before sending them back*, he thought.

Finally, the buses filled. As they moved away slowly, Jeff remembered his last bus ride from the base to the airport. There had been antiwar protesters near the airport entrance, shouting slogans and throwing eggs and tomatoes at the buses as they moved past.

The thunder of jets roaring overhead brought Jeff back to reality. Several low explosions came from far away. He looked toward their direction, but not being able to see anything, he slumped into his seat and closed his eyes.

A few minutes later, the bus stopped, he opened his eyes to the sound of men's voices and saw a large sign that read *Processing Center*. He looked down through the window, and saw soldiers standing behind a fenced area.

Sweat continued to run down the sides of his face. This was something he knew he would have to learn to deal with. He wiped the liquid away with his index finger, flicking it at the floor. The crowd at the fence cheered as the Marines began leaving the bus.

"What's this all about?" Jeff asked the Marine beside him.

"We must be their replacements. It sure must feel good knowing you're finally leaving. Some day, we'll be standing there, cheering for the new arrivals, too."

"I hope so."

They filed out of the bus and into a large hangar with a high ceiling and poor ventilation. The heat became more intensified by large ceiling fans producing swirls of hot air directly down onto the seating area.

Jeff followed the other men into the seats. By now, his green shirt was dark green from excessive perspiration. He seated himself in a chair that was of little comfort.

A single Marine Officer, dressed in camouflage material, including a jungle hat and spit shine polished boots, stood on the platform facing the group. Everyone was silent. He looked down at the sheets of paper in his hands, and then raised his head to face the new arrivals. There was no perspiration on his exposed skin or clothing. He scanned the group as if looking for someone in particular, and then he brought his gaze back to the middle of the group. Without a PA system, loudly he called out.

"The United States Marine Corps welcomes you to Da Nang." His rough voice echoed throughout the hangar. "Those of you coming here for the first time may find life's conditions a little to the extreme, long rainy seasons and heat showing no mercy. Biting insects will love your fresh blood, as you will be prepared to deal with them. Winters aren't much better. In mid-winter when the temperature reaches its lowest point, around 70 degrees, your coat may be your best friend. Don't take anything for granted. One last word on this subject, value your issued gear. You only get one set." He held up one finger for all to see, and then repeated himself, "one set!"

Jeff sat thinking. *No mercy is right. It's gonna be a long hard and rough road until the day I leave this place.*

"As you know," he hesitated. "There's a war going on around us, twenty-four hours a day." He bent to retrieve a small box. In exchange, he placed the papers on the floor near his feet. "Use your training wisely, and you have a good chance of leaving here alive. There are only three planes leaving here everyday. You create your own choice."

He took a flat piece of green plastic from the box. It unrolled into a six-foot bag, he held it up for all to see. "One plane carries the dead. Don't go out there trying to being a hero. This is one of the planes you might wind-up returning home on."

He dropped the body bag and reached into the box to pull out a half-empty plasma bag. The tube ending danced on the platform. "Another plane carries the disabled. Most of these people failed, and I do mean failed, to obey orders. Unfortunately, these are the lucky ones, they get a second chance at life."

He dropped the plasma bag and pulled out a plane ticket. "The last plane. I repeat myself. The last plane." He remained silent for a few seconds, "is the one you count your days for. Most Marines would sell their soul for one of these tickets. Need I say anything further?"

No one spoke a word.

An enlisted Marine approached the platform, and the officer walked off. The enlisted man raised a small stack of papers waist high and looked at the group.

"When your name's called, answer and come forward. Your unit has sent transportation. The first group to leave will be heading for Hill 327 and Happy Valley. Listen up for your name." He started reciting the names in alphabetical order.

Adams rises, walked away. Low chatter started up between the new arrivals. Jeff relaxed in his seat. He saw a piece of newspaper at his feet and picked it up to use as a fan against the heat. The additional waves of hot air didn't help. A stream of sweat raced down the side of his face. He stopped to wipe perspiration from his eyes. *If anything*, he thought, *I'd probably die of dehydration.*

Barren, rises, walks away.

Another Marine seated next to him, wiped his face and neck with a rag. "Your first trip?" He asked.

Several jets raced past the hangar at low altitude, causing everyone to stop talking. The sonic boom, echoing throughout the hangar sounded like a major explosion, Jeff jump. There was immediate silence for a moment, and then the enlisted man went back to calling off names. Jeff had forgotten the question.

"I'm sorry," he said. "What did you say?"

"Is this your first trip?"

Jeff sees Correll rise and walk away.

"Yeah, I can think of other places I'd rather be."

Jeff returns the newspaper to the floor.

"I can see the war got you jumping already and you haven't even gotten to the bush."

"I'll learn to deal with it when the time comes."

"It's not that bad in the bush. This is my second trip."

Jeff looked at him in amazement. "You like it here that much?"

Finney rises, walked away.

"Yeah, there's nothing like being in the bush and living off the land."

The expression on the man's face frightened Jeff. He could see the man's veins starting to pop up, and with that came a lust for blood in his eyes.

Jeff tried to remain calm. "You mean eating fruits, vegetables and small animals?"

The man became hyper and moved his hands all around wildly. "No, not that crap, raiding V.C. villages and taking what you want."

Harley rises, walked away.

"That's not living off the land. The Marine opened his mouth to speak. Jeff shot his hand straight up in the air in an effort to stop him. "Did you just hear what the Captain said about being a hero?"

The man squeezed his head with both hands. "That's a bunch of bull. Do you really believe that mess?"

"Yeah, ain't that what we was taught back in boot camp?"

"They got your head all screwed up. Listen, you gotta do whatever it takes to survive. You and your buddies are on your own. Death is always in your next step. You can get wounded or killed anywhere in this country at a moment's notice, combat or not. We always say, 'ever man who dies in this country is a hero.' That's our motto, because we, as Americans, are fighting for their cause. There ain't gonna be no big celebration for you when you leave here. And nobody's gonna put something extra in your pay check for doing a better job than the next guy by risking your life. If anything, you'll be ridiculed for being here."

Jeff was starting to think; *maybe this man had a point.* The word 'ridiculed' made him think about his father's opposition to the war.

"Anyway, check this out." He took his hands down. "When you stay in the bush, two, three, four months at a time, you'll learn what it's all about. Use Charlie's tricks on Charlie, and what's gonna make the fun so exciting," his expression changed to a happy mood, "it's all part of team work with your buddies. Try sneaking up on some Viet Cong." The man twisted around in his seat to face Jeff. His eyes widen." Catch 'em alive, string 'em up, and cut them into small pieces. It's all legal murder over here you know, regardless of what you've been told. Make them beg before dying. They do the same to Marines."

Livingston rises, walked away.

Jeff was ready to relocate. He had heard enough. "This ain't just exactly what I was expecting to hear. I'm in supply. I don't hardly think I'll be sneaking up on anyone."

"Legal murder, or make 'em beg to die?"

"Do you think they sent you out here to bag groceries?"

"Neither one, I don't know if I can kill anyone."

"You will. All Marines are taught to kill. It's in your blood, and you haven't even realized it. Wait until you've been here awhile."

"Nope, I refuse to believe that."

"It's kill or be killed. Look at it this way. Your patrol and Charlie's patrol going on a hunting trips in the bush," he threw his hands up in the air, "and there ain't no rules, none what so ever."

Jeff wondered how long has this man had been this crazy.

"THE Geneva convention has articles of war that everyone must follow."

"Man, you ain't listening. The only Geneva Charlie knows is his woman."

"Jeff Richards!" came the call from the enlisted man.

Jeff jumped to his feet and stared down at the Marine but couldn't think of anything else to say.

"Jeff Richards?" the Marine's voice grew louder. His head slowly turned in search of the individual.

"Here, Sir." Jeff looked forward.

The Marine brought his attention back to Jeff. "Get up here, Soldier!" he shouted. "There's too many names to be called for me to be repeating myself."

Jeff moved away from his seat.

"Hope to meet up with you in the bush," the seated Marine said.

When Jeff reached the aisle, he gave the seated Marine one final glance. The Marine winked and presented a thumb's up. Jeff returned the sign with one of his own. "Not if I can help it," he said, in a low voice.

Jeff casually made his way to the processing table and was given a set of papers to be signed. He did so without reading them and gave them back. The private behind the table looked through a long box filled with large envelopes, and then took one out. After looking at Jeff's signature, he handed the envelope to him, and then pointed toward a side door. "Get your sea bag out there."

Jeff returned to the smoldering heat. The thermometer on the face of the hangar read *111.* Jeff looked at his wristwatch. It was nine o'clock in the morning. He joined the Marines waiting to be transported to their outfits.

A well-built lance corporal dressed in a jungle uniform, web boots, and a pistol strapped to his side, came to lead the group to a storage baggage area.

Jeff learned from boot camp, the military way of piling seabags was to form a pyramid. Usually, any bags lying at the bottom ended up with some sort of broken items. He was careful not to pack anything breakable. He watched as the men began removing their bags. Finally, his bag was uncovered. A large, glossy green **X,** running down the side of his bag, stood out among the pile. He pulled it off to one side.

CHAPTER TWO

The uncovered military transport truck rolled along a narrow, two-lane dirt road filled with Marines at a fast clip. Its large tires fanned dust outwards onto the various Vietnamese people moving alongside the road. All of them seemed to be carrying, pulling, or pushing objects. A few young girls waved to the riders. No one aboard waved back.

The truck continued to roll onward through a vast region of open rice fields. Jeff sat near the back of the truck. A constant flow of warm air flowed past him, drying a portion of his sweat-stained clothing. He loosened several buttons on his utility jacket and laid his arms across the back railing and relaxed. He watched the scenery pass by.

After seeing several travelers, he realized all the natives wore pajama style suits in combination colors of black and white. Small children, mostly boys, wore tops and straw hats but had nothing around their legs.

How strange, he thought. *Almost nobody wears anything on his feet.*

Those who did wore slippers that reminded him of thongs for the shower. Friendly women waved to the truck as it rolled along. This time Jeff waved back. Several fully armed squads of soldiers appeared, forging their way through a vast field of water pools. That reminded Jeff of the fish farms back home in Louisiana.

Louisiana was never this hot and dusty, he thought.

The scenery became more picturesque. Small trees with healthy leaves sat isolated along the banks beside the pools. Older children walked on the banks carrying straw baskets over their heads.

The truck finally arrived at a closed gate manned by armed military police. One of them stepped from the small booth and looked at the driver. He immediately started walking along side the truck, looking up at the seated men. After approaching the rear, he climbed high enough to look across the floor, then came down, and returned to the booth. With a sudden nod of his head, which represented a jester for the driver to enter, another military policeman opened the gate.

The truck rolled into the compound, which was surrounded by a double row of tall, chain link fence and topped with swirling Constantine wires. Barbed wire ran through there center's as far as the eye could see. Dense vegetation concealed the base from beyond the perimeter. Bunkers, sticking out of the ground two to three feet high and covered with many layers of sand bags, could be seen every where along the truck's route as it slowly moved toward headquarters. Jeff took a good look at the many low buildings surrounded by layers upon layers of discolored sandbags. A water truck moved around the compound, spraying down the loose dirt to keep down the dust.

Marines armed with rifles and loaded cartridge belts filled with magazines walked freely throughout the area. A few trustworthy Vietnamese workers shuffled from one place to another with badges hanging around their necks by strings. There was no shade from the hot sun except for inside the buildings. Not a tree had grown anywhere within the compound as far as Jeff could see from where he sat. Rows of single floor huts lined both sides of the road, six deep. Behind them, a Sea Bee crew labored in constructing more huts.

As the truck rolled past a sports court, a small group of soldiers in shirts and skins, gently moved about on the basketball court. Despite the heat, they seemed to be having fun. Several gunships raced overhead at low altitude. One of the gunners sitting beside an open doorway waved with one hand while keeping the other on his M-60 machine gun.

Jeff waved back, but it was too late for the gunner to see him as the gunship swiftly moved out of sight.

What a place, he thought. *Guys from all walks of life and every State united in one huge remote location for the purpose to assist in stopping oppression. It feels strange actually being in a real war. I'm always going to expect something to happen without a moment's notice. I can see what that crazy nut back at the hangar was trying to drive home on me. I'm starting to feel something. What is there to stop something from flying over that fence? And Look at these people, just as calm as can be. I find it hard to believe this base, deep in the middle of a war zone, looks like it has never been invaded.*

Jeff's thoughts were suddenly interrupted when several explosions echoed through the air. He quickly turned to see several bellowing thick clouds of smoke far off, rising toward the sky. This made him a little nervous but he kept his composure.

The truck stopped before the compound's main office, which was Headquarters. The driver jumped down and made his way to the rear where he unfastened the tailgate, allowing it to flop with a loud bang. "This is it! First and last stop. Everybody out." He paused a moment. "This is one of the safest bases around."

Jeff was partially covered by a layer of mud and dust from a combination of sweat and dirt. He jumped down, and his knees almost kissed the roadway. He pulled his sea bag onto his shoulder, carried it to the doorway, and dropped it to rest against the building.

Inside the office, a private first class in his early thirties, held the receiving end of a field phone to his ear. "Jeff Richards has arrived, send someone to deliver him to his unit." There was a moment of silence. The Marine became annoyed with his response. His face glowed with anger. "I know you guys got somebody goofing off over there...I don't care, send him...I would appreciate it if he could be picked up before lunch." He slammed the receiver down and immediately began talking at random. "I have never seen such lazy guys, hating to do their job. Have a seat. Transportation coming."

Jeff eyeballed the room. For a field office, most of the equipment was up to date. It was capable of manning five men in a comfortable setting with desk room to spare. A section near the rear was closed off for officers. While Jeff sat quietly eyeballing, his eyes came to rest on a private trying to get any clear reception from a radio sitting on his desk. Finally, the man gave up and sat the unit inside his desk drawer.

All this time Jeff waited patiently for his guide to a supply unit. Suddenly, the door opened, and a well-built, stocky Caucasian Marine with a deep suntan entered. His attire resembled that of a John Wayne combat movie, sagging cartridge belt to one side and a camouflage helmet, slightly cocked backward.

Jeff recognized Vick right away. They were friends on another base. Vick came to him, they laughed and shook hands.

"I see they pulled your number," Vick said. "What a lucky break to get shipped here."

"Yeah," Jeff replied. "I finally made it. If I had to come, somebody was looking out for me to be with you."

Vick's feelings began to show signs of excitement. "My man, we gonna have good times like you ain't never saw before."

"He's all yours," the private said. "I'm sorry to see such a young man come to a sorry outfit like yours. Get him geared up, fed, and rested." He pointed to Vick. "Go light on the good times. Make sure he's sober enough to report for duty in the morning. The captain might want to see him first thing."

Vick pretended to be surprised. "You talking to me?"

"Yup, I'm talking to you."

"Give me a break. This is his first day in Country. We ought to make him feel right at home."

"Just make sure he can stand at attention. Don't start him off on the wrong foot."

Vick laughed, and then turned to Jeff. "It's great to see you, let's get out of here. These guys have no sense of humor during working hours." They started toward the door. "He's just jealous because he can't be one of us, welcome to Unpleasant Pastures."

Jeff stood wondering what that meant, but this wasn't the right time to ask. "Thanks," he said, in a casual manor.

They stood motionless on the walkway in front of the Headquarters' building breathing the smothering heated air while Vick surveyed the area. Jeff turned to Vick. "Did you really think they would let me miss out on this war?"

"If they did, you'd be the first."

"I'll take your bag," offered Vick.

Jeff pointed to it. Vick plucked it up, took it to his Jeep. Jeff stared off in a different direction. Vick boldly slammed it into the back seat. He looked back and saw Jeff. "Come on, you can't see everything from that spot." Jeff climbed into the front seat and Vick drove off.

Jeff pulled at his undershirt, which was soaked with sweat and sticking to his chest. "How do you stand the heat?"

Vick pushed at the front of his helmet. "It wasn't easy at first, but, after your skin gets about six shades darker, it's easier to take."

"Looks like I'll be frying for a while."

Vick eyed Jeff's skin and smiled.

Jeff had a feeling Vick was in a good mood. Now was a good time to ask him what he meant about this place being Unpleasant Pastures. "You got me thinking, tell me something."

"Anything for a friend."

"At the Processing Center, they called this place Happy

Valley, you call it Unpleasant Pastures. What's up with that?"

"In due time my friend, you will come to know this place as such, seeing is believing."

"Maybe so."

They pulled into a parking area adjacent to the living quarters. A narrow walkway stretched across a plane of sand, branching off toward each individual hut.

The Jeep moved slowly as the two sat and baked in the hot sun.

"We've got a spare bed where I'm staying," Vick said. "The dude who had it last, boarded the same plane you just got off. Worldley was a happy go lucky dude."

"Those were one happy bunch of dudes waiting to leave. That would be great to stay at your place. You can show me the ropes."

The Jeep stopped. Vick lifted his hands from the steering wheel and leaned back against the hard seat. "This is it, hooch ninety-one." Vick pointed in the direction of the hut.

Jeff's eyes followed in the pointed direction.

This hut was no different from the others. Its floor set eighteen inches or more from a plain of course sand mounted on wooden piles. The walls were constructed with the lower half comprised of four foot high sheets of thick plywood and the upper portion covered in a fine mesh screen to aide in ventilation. A single layer of faded sandbags covered the entire A framed roof. At both ends, a full screen door was constructed to provide easy accent and departure. In big numbers, a 91 was hand painted over the doorway.

Jeff laughed. "Hooch? That sounds like some rotgut whiskey we drank back in old J-ville."

Vick turned toward him and placed an arm across the back of his seat.

"Those were good days, getting wasted across the tracks on homemade white lightning."

"It was like fire going down," Jeff said. "But it sure hit the spot. I use to pinch my noise while drinking it to keep from being knocked out."

"That was the only way you could drink it. Here's to good old J'ville."

They gave each other the high five, and then they were silent for a moment.

"This place is crazy," Vick said. "Grass grows freely everywhere. Whiskey sells for five dollars a quart."

Jeff's jaw dropped in amazing surprise. "Grass grows freely? Here? On this base?"

"No, not on the base that I know of, out in the bush."

"Some crazy dude at the Processing Center was raveling off about the bush. He wasn't talking about grass. It was all about living off the land. I believe he could have been a pot head just hallucinating."

"I wouldn't be surprised. A lot of these dudes living in the bush got real mental problems."

"We spraying this Agent Orange stuff that's only suppose to be killing vegetation. All the fellows walking around in it."

"What about us on this compound"

"We cool. That mess is probably happening up North."

"That dude had to be from the North. He did right by coming back here. Somebody in the States would take him out real quick. You should of heard him, and those wild eyes."

"I wouldn't worry about them until the war is over. Most of them either getting killed or defect."

"That's a shame. I hear a lot of them defect."

"Yeah, later we'll hitch a ride to Hill 327."

"What's over there?"

"That's where the PX is hidden. You can pick up some free grass along the way."

"You mean we can stop anywhere and pick it?"

Vick laughed. "No, the VC have people packaging the stuff and throwing it into our trucks along the route. You really into this grass stuff aren't you?'"

"Sort of. I never saw grass growing on plants, or got it for free." Jeff looked at him suspiciously. "Is the stuff on?"

"Where you from?"

"A little hick town in Louisiana."

"Grass is the plant. It's the best. I think they discovered it."

"You pulling my leg, it's free?"

"Believe what I say. The Vietnamese people know better then to cross an American. War has no rules."

"That's the second time I heard that today. That ain't what they say back in the States."

"Yes it is. You just don't realize it. It's the same all over the world. Try talking to a dude about rules when he's pointing a gun in your face when the smoke clears. I guarantee you won't be the one standing."

Jeff had to think about it for a moment. "I guess you're right when you put it that way."

They climbed out of the Jeep. Perspiration ran down the sides of Jeff's face and dripped from his chin. He went to stand on the walkway and Vick pulled the sea bag from the Jeep, slung it over his shoulder, and then led Jeff to the hut.

The squeaking screen door reminded Jeff of an old haunted house. He followed Vick down a narrow aisle. The ceiling was slanted so low; the interior needed lighting most of the time to aide the men in seeing.

Vick sat the seabag beside a double bunk. The bottom was made, showing someone resided there. The top was nothing but a worn mattress and a few loose papers scattered over it. Vick removed the papers and sat them on the bunk below.

"Here's home looking at you, "Vick said, while making

a sweeping gesture with his hand. "Top bunk, best view of the area."

"If it's got to be this way, so be it." Jeff looked around. A few rows away, a young Marine lay sleeping in just his shorts on a top bunk. A small portable fan attached to the side of the hut blew warm air over the upper portion of his body. Pictures and other personal items hung neatly beside many bunks.

"Here's a little advice."

"Shoot."

"Sleep with your head close to the aisle. The breeze from people coming down the aisle ain't much but it feels good. Other then that, this place is like an oven turned to broiler."

"Point well taken. I'm beginning to feel it. Some place you got here." Jeff sat on the lower bunk.

"It ain't like back home," Vick said. "But it comes close. This place really comes alive at night. The soul brothers be jammin heavy. There's no end to the nightly partying in this hut."

Jeff had that curious look on his face. "Wait a minute. There's a war going on out there. Do you guys ever think about it?"

Vick showed no concern. "The war is no big thing to us. You see Mash on TV?"

"Yeah."

"Same boat, different location." He glanced at his watch. "Let's get over to supply before lunch. It's not safe around here without your gear. You never know when Charlie might get enough opium in him to try taking us out."

"So there is some combat you guys engage it."

Vick seemed shy about answering. "Let me put it to you this way. Only a few dudes are assigned to a night squad. Their job is mainly to patrol the base perimeter. Stop the V.C. from sneaking onto this base and doing damage."

"What's my chance of getting called?"

"Chances of getting called looks pretty slim. You can put your name down at Headquarters, but don't expect any word for at lease three to four months down the road."

"I got time. I might just do that. Something I can write home about."

Vick gave him one of those crazy looks. "Don't count on any real hard core action. They do a little shooting up every now and then, mostly at noises in the dark. I know because I've been there." Vick's facial expression took on a dramatic change. "But the rocket attacks is the ones you gotta watch out for. They keep you on the run."

Jeff remained silent. Vick's face began to brighten. "Come on. Let's head out. There's a lot to see."

They went back to the Jeep, and Vick drove off.

The Jeep rolled along the dirt road, lifting a cloud of dust behind it. Minutes later, they parked beside a large warehouse. Several Marines in T-shirts and dog tags labored to repair a wide opening on the side of the building.

Vick jumped out and headed toward the entrance. Jeff hurried to catch up.

Inside, a crew gathered and placed a variety of loose items from the floor onto shelves.

Jeff's jaw dropped when he saw the destruction.

Vick covered his mouth to conceal a burst of laughter. He and Jeff walked toward a long counter that stretched from one side of the building to the other.

Bending over the counter was a tall, slender Marine dressed in a newly pressed camouflage jungle outfit. His dog tags lay partly on the counter as he filled out a form. The presents of Jeff and Vick gave him just cause to stop writing.

Vick lowered his hand, but his smile remained.

Jeff failed to see what was so funny.

"Charlie putting you guys to work?" asked Vick.

The corporal behind the counter was not in a good mood. "Yeah, they damn near hit the building, came pretty close."

"You know what they say about horseshoes, explosives and hand grenades," said Vick. "Close is as good as a hit."

"I agree. As far as I'm concerned, the building was hit, but the Captain don't think so."

"What does he know? He's just a paper pusher."

The corporal eyed Jeff. "What can I do for you?"

"Meet Jeff," Vick said. "We were stationed together in North Carolina before I came to this sorry place."

"Hi, Jeff, I'm Sam."

"Hi," Jeff replied.

Vick held one hand near the side of his mouth and looked around to see if anyone was watching them. Then brought his eyes to a fixed stare into Sam's eyes." He started to softly whisper to him. "Hook up my man. Give him all new stuff. You know how we do."

"Sure," Sam said, trying to keep his voice low. "Any friend of Vick's is a friend of mine. Nothing but the best for Vick's friends." He walked off.

"I'm very grateful," said Jeff. He surveyed the minor destruction. "How often does this happen?"

"At least three times a week."

Jeff was caught off guard with this shocking news. "Three times a week?" He asked in amazement.

"I was only joking."

"You almost scared me half to death."

"Let me correct that. Everybody knows that I like to joke around a lot. They were lucky this time. Most of the time, the VC miss everything. The whole camp"

Sam returned with his hands full of weaponry and gear. "Tell Jeff about the time Charlie hit the food dump." He set down the stuff and walked off again.

Vick laughed. Jeff smiled and waited.

"That was funny," Vick said. "Charlie must've had only one rocket that night. They only fire 'em at night-that's why they usually miss. Anyway, the thing went through the roof and hit a couple pallets of pickles."

They laughed.

Jeff was cracking up so hard; he reached down to hold his side.

"Yeah. We had pickle juice smelling for almost a month."

"After seven days, we started wearing gas masks. The smell got pretty ripe in the heat."

Sam returned with a footlocker and bedding, stacking them on top of the counter. "I believe this is everything. The best of whatever we got in the house. If you're not satisfied with any item, bring it back in a couple of weeks when the new shipment arrives." He looked over the list, pulled a receiving list from under the counter, and pushed it toward Jeff. "Put your John Hancock on the dotted line, and then you're on your way."

Jeff quickly scanned over the item. "I see no problem with this. Thanks for the offer." He signed, and then he and Vick gathered the items and carried them toward the door.

"See you at the card game tonight!" Sam called to Vick.

"You bet, don't be late, seats go fast."

Jeff whispered to Vick, "you some kind of card shark?" Before Vick could answer, Sam called out. "I'll be the first one there."

Vick spoke to Jeff in a low voice. "See for yourself."

They loaded the Jeep and drove off. As the Jeep traveled back toward the hut, they passed the water truck spraying the opposite side of the road.

Once back at the hut, they carried Jeff's things inside. Jeff slammed the items on top of his bed while Vick slid the footlocker underneath.

"I have to report back to my J-O-B," Vick said. "Wait here. I'll be right back, then we can split for lunch." Jeff nodded his head in agreement.

"Cool, my last meal was a bag of those airplane peanuts that wasn't even a mouth full and a six ounce plastic glass of soda."

"I know the feeling", Vick said, while nodding his head. "I've been there many times."

Vick went to his sleeping area, put something in his pocket, and walked out of the hut.

CHAPTER THREE

After Jeff finished making his bed, he placed the contents of his seabag in his footlocker. *I'll rest until Vick returns*, he thought.

Just as he made himself comfortable, two African-American Marines entered the hut. They looked like something out of a combat movie. Both wearing a helmet with chinstraps moving loosely under their chins. Each wore a bullet proof vest and sported a rifle across his shoulder. A fully loaded cartridge belt sagged to one side under its own weight.

The tall, lanky darker Marine seemed in more of a hurry than the shorter, lighter man, who almost ran to keep up. Their conversation started the moment they entered the hut.

"You shot a water buffalo?" The lanky Marine asked, shaking his head in disbelief. "Are you crazy?"

They stopped at the bed across from Jeff and acted as if he was invisible. Jeff propped himself up on one arm to watch. The shorter Marine began to move his hands as if trying to justify his actions.

"He was charging at me! You think I'll let something that big and dumb hurt me?"

The other man knelt before his footlocker and started working the combination. "That's still a dumb animal.

You should have moved to one side to let him pass. Now that's a five hundred dollar fine. More money, thrown away. Think some time." He removed the lock, opened the top as far back as the catch would allow, and took a stack of money from a transparent container. "Here!" The shorter man broke out into a smile upon receiving the money. The other man didn't seem pleased about giving up the money. "If I don't supply you, you'll never have any bread." A shy, shifty expression came over him while staring at the shorter man. "You owe me, remember it."

The shorter man seemed indignant. "Since when have I failed to pay you? I thought we were tight?"

"We are. It just gets to me when you don't use good judgment."

"Don't be cracking on me like that. Everybody's entitled to a few mistakes."

Rich became angry, "a few mistakes! You already exceeded your limit. I just don't know about you anymore." He locked the footlocker and pushed it under the bed.

They stopped talking and walked toward the door. The shorter Marine, who was following only took a few steps before stopping when he spotted Jeff. "Damn," he said, in a sarcastic manner. "They work fast. Worldley's bed didn't even get cold before they packed another dude in it."

Jeff didn't reply. The tall Marine was outside by now, the short man ran to catch up.

Jeff got off the bunk and walked around the bunks, passing the sleeping Marine. He stopped at a makeshift nightstand, where a picture in a folder caught his eye. He picked it up. It showed a Marine his age in dress blues sitting in a chair holding twin girls, one on each knee. An extremely beautiful woman stood beside him.

He set down the picture. Next to it was a calendar with rows of crossed off days. *I guest this is what he said about the plane ticket*, he thought.

Jeff heard the sound of a Jeep pulling up close the hut.

Vick jumps from the Jeep and heads down the walkway.

Jeff hurried back into the center aisle, then walked slowly toward his area.

Vick walked in through the squeaking door. "Sun's blazing, heat stroke season for new comers. It's gonna be one of those hot ones." He removed his helmet. Sweat ran down his neck and into his clothes.

Jeff wasn't at all happy. "I can hardly breathe."

"This ain't nothing. Some days, it gets around 125 in the shade. Believe my word, that's in the shade. But you'll get used to it."

"I doubt it. Say, what's the chance of getting some ice?"

Vick threw up his hand in an act of being thrown off guard. "Ice, Woo. No such animal. People around here would kill for one single cube. I got the rest of the day off. Let's get some grub, and then I'll show you around."

"Show me someplace where the temperature's pleasant." Vick said.

"You're in it. When again, you'll love winter here. When it gets around 70 degrees, you'll need a coat."

"I doubt that also."

"Seeing is believing."

Vick laughed and patted Jeff's shoulder, Jeff smiled. "Let's go," Vick said.

Jeff grabbed his helmet and bullet proof vest. The mess hall was nearby. They walked to it quickly, and to Jeff it looked like another warehouse from the outside. Inside, they passed a man counting those who entered, and then they emerged into a vast area of bodies and dirty tables. There were two lines of men waiting to be served.

Vick and Jeff joined one line, and it slowly moved forward. They got there rations, and Jeff located a vacant table. He and Vick set the dirty trays off to one side.

"No matter what mess hall I eat in," Jeff said. "They all seem to be the same, dirty tables with trays everywhere."

"What do you expect when you're dining with a bunch of animals. Remember boot camp?"

"Yeah, how can I ever forget? Every other day somebody was calling our platoon a herd."

Vick broke out into a burst of laughter. Jeff could only smile.

"Marines are taught to eat quick, fast, and in a hurry," Jeff commented. "At least I know I was."

Vick replied, "You mean like pigs. They don't cleanup, they eat up."

Jeff laughed. "That, too. Do you think we're suppose to eat without tasting it?"

"I try to."

They began to eat.

Jeff ate a small amount, and then looked up. "Who's this dude Worldley?"

Vick looked surprised. "You know him?"

"No, not that I can recall." He lowered his head and toyed with his food. "Who told you about Worldley?" "Two brothers came into the hut while you were gone. They said something about me moving into his spot and the bed wasn't even cold."

Vick looked at him curiously. "What did the dudes look like?"

"One was tall and lanky, a little on the dark side, and the other, a little shorter with a slightly lighter complexion. Both dressed down in combat gear looking like G.I. Joe."

"They stopped across from you?"

"Yeah." Jeff stuffed a small portion of food into his mouth. Now Jeff became curious. "Somebody hot on you trail?"

Vick relaxed, and then laughed. "Never my good

friend. That was Rich and Terry, two con artist. They're always up to something." He leaned forward and pointed at Jeff. "Watch yourself around them. If you ever give 'em anything, kiss it good-bye. Worldley's been gone a week. I keep getting this feeling they ripped him off real good. They were probably testing you."

"How's that?"

"They intentionally allowed you to ease drop in on one of their schemes. Did they talk loud?"

Jeff looked surprised. "Yeah, the conversation pertained to a water buffalo and some money. They acted as though I wasn't there."

"Oh, they knew. Give 'em a couple of days to get to really know you and they'll be asking you to lend them something."

"Thanks for schooling me. I'm no sucker. They want to get down with the games, we can get it on."

"Worldley was the type of dude who would give you his last. Just before he left, he told me somebody broke into his footlocker and took several thousand dollars."

"That's funny. While I was laying on my bunk, the tall one gave the other one some money from his footlocker."

Vick banged his fist against the table. He had that wild look in his eyes. "They probably took it. I can't think of anybody else." Vick held Jeff's attention during a moment of silence. "Ted, no. Bob, no. It must have been them."

"Well, Worldley's gone now. Let it ride."

Vick thought about it for a moment. He began to calm down. "Yeah, you're right. He's gone, but I'm not gonna forget it."

They finished eating. Jeff couldn't compare the food with anything he had ever tasted before. It tasted bad, but, if everyone ate it, he couldn't complain. On the way out, they disposed of their trays and silverware.

They walked alongside the road, and it was hotter than before. Jeff lifted his helmet to shake out the mounting sweat accumulated in his hair and replaced his helmet.

"Let's go into the village," Vick said. "I'll show you around and give you some schooling on the happenings. First, you never leave the base without being fully armed. You never know when you might have to use it. Secondly, don't second guest the natives. They act friendly, but most of them aren't."

They went to their hut and gathered up their war gear, and then caught an open-bed truck headed for Hill 327. Many villagers walked along the roadside, and the truck rolled forward. A large cloud of smoke appeared from a far. Small groups of helicopters, barely seen, appeared to be headed toward that location from different directions. Jeff turned away to see a bunch of Vietnamese up ahead. When the truck came near the group, people began throwing something wrapped in plastic into the open bay of the truck area.

Jeff watched as Vick and the others started collecting the plastic bags. After noticing they resembled cigarettes, Jeff joined the group.

The truck hit a stretch of bumpy road and it began bouncing so much that all the men were flying everywhere within the confined area. The packs looked like frogs jumping up and down, too. Once, Jeff was bounced so hard he was almost thrown from the truck, that frightened him. He grabbed the wooden seat as if his life depended on it, trying to seat himself with three plastic packages in his hand. The other riders seemed as thought they had been down this road several times and knew how to handle this treatment.

Finally, he managed to get seated. A sigh of relief came over him. He watched Vick and the others bounce a few more times before they returned to their seats, too.

Vick smiled. "Just like riding a wild stallion. Having fun?"

Jeff didn't smile back. He was still feeling the effects of his ordeal. "I think the trip's a little scary." He looked down at the packages he almost got hurt trying to grab. Inside each was ten neatly rolled marijuana sticks. He set them in his trouser pocket.

Vick moved closer to Jeff. "This is good smoke. Wait until you fire these babies up." Suddenly, Vick had a thought. *He gave me the impression he had been fooling around with this stuff before by his actions, but is he really down with it? I'd better check him out before I expose my whole hand.* "Do you smoke?" Vick calmly asked.

Jeff had a feeling of expression on his face that almost frightened Vick. "Yeah man, I'd smoke up Mexico if I could."

Vick felt a sense of relief.

The truck struck a pothole. Jeff was quick to grab the railing behind him. "Can't they do something about this road?" Jeff asked. "I feel like a jumping jack."

"Not really. Charlie likes planting mines on it. This is the famous Ho Chi Minh Trail leading from one end of the country to the other. It's the road most traveled by military trucks."

"I don't care who's trail it is. This is the pits. I feel like a jumping jack."

Vick laughed. "It's not who's, its Ho. There's a lot you'll have to get used to, you're funny. You should blend in well."

"I hope so."

Approaching the outdoor market, Jeff sees its surroundings are filled with small huts and rice patties.

Finally, the truck stopped at a small roadside market between the compound and Hill 327. Jeff stared at what was before him.

"This is the village," said Vick.

Vick, Jeff, and some of the others jumped onto the roadway. The truck rolled off with the reminding riders. From a distance, the place looked like a yard sale. As the men moved closer, Jeff saw two paths going behind the item covered tables. Everything sat above a clean, dirt floor. Trees loomed overhead, providing shade to the venders and their customers.

Soldiers dressed in combat gear browsed the tables along with a few Vietnamese shoppers. Some spoke broken Vietnamese. Others used English and sign language in conjunction to get there message across.

Vick took the lead as they entered the area.

"Watch these people," Vick said. "They can spot a newcomer right off. Don't let 'em buffalo you into buying stolen junk."

They walked slowly, looking at table after table until stopping at a small stand where a Vietnamese lady was sitting selling sodas.

"Hey, Vick!" Said a middle-aged Vietnamese woman wearing a wide straw-hat, white shirt, and black pajama bottoms. She smiled at him. "You want buy Coca-Cola! Bery, bery cold."

Jeff was surprised. "They're selling soda from the States in the middle of this Jungle! Is this something I should believe?"

"They can get stuff you can't find in the PX. They've got a heck of a black market. You want one?"

Jeff nodded with a yes jester, and Vick held up two fingers. "Give me two Colas, bery cold."

She moved from her sitting position to a chest. "You want two?"

He nodded again.

She lifted the top all the way up. Jeff's eyes grew larger upon viewing the ice inside. "I've seen it all now," he said in delight. "They got ice, too."

"Yup," Vick responded. "They got it all."

"You want two," she repeated.

Vick raised two fingers. "One for me. One for my friend."

She set two bottles on the table before them. "Four dolla," she blurred out while blinking. Vick stood looking at her. She seemed to be growing impatient. Signs of anger set in on her face. "No play games. You want! Four dolla." She worked her fingers back and forth.

Vick raised his hands. "What's this, a stick up? Last week it was three dolla! And two fifty week before."

"Hard get." She turned her eyes away. "Price go up. Supply bery, bery low." Her fingers worked back and forth as she extended her hand. "Four dolla. I no ask gain."

Vick took a roll of mixed, Vietnamese and American, bills from his back pocket, peeled off four Vietnamese dollars, and set them in her hand. She put them under the counter. Vick took the sodas and gave Jeff one.

"Mama-san, you rob me." He looked at her.

She looked right back. "I know. What you American say, law of supply and demon."

"You got that right, demon. You know this is highway robbery."

Jeff began to get a little uneasy. "You better go light on her. She might want to send you a flaring rocket tonight."

"Knowing her, she just might for four dollars."

Vick turned the bottle upside down and ran his finger around the center of the bottom. He held it up and eyed the contents carefully.

The woman went back to sitting in her chair again.

"Some things I examine closer than others," Vick said. "Especially, when it comes down to my health. One of my buddies found a mouse in his bottle. Check it out before you open it."

Jeff examined the top of the bottle. "How in the heck do you get a mouse down through that small hole?"

"You don't."

Vick pointed to the resealed bottom of the bottle. "They fill the bottle by cutting a hole in the bottom, then reseal it."

"I'll be darn, very clever move."

"This way they can put anything they want inside."

Vick sipped, swished it around in his mouth, and

swallowed. Satisfied that the taste was correct, he held up the bottle to salute the woman. "Mama-san, if this stuff kills me, I'll come back to get you."

She adjusted herself in her seat. "I neber sell bad tuff, this good tuff, I no lie. You die, blame America."

Jeff thought their conversation was the funniest thing. He performed a short laugh. At some point, he suppressed his laughter and held the bottle close to his face. Not being able to see anything inside, he opened it and took a swallow. "Real stuff," he said in delight. "Just like back home."

Vick was ready to move on. "Let's walk," he said as he surveyed the area.

They walked away to a secluded area in the shade and stopped. Jeff sipped on his soda like it was a baby's bottle. Vick took a piece of cloth from his back pocket to swab his face with, and returned it to the same pocket.

"You say you don't trust these people?"

"When you've been here long enough, some of these people grow on you. At times you think of them as friendly people."

"I'll have to weigh that thought."

"I only trust them on some things. Sodas. I see them drinking them so I take a chance on drinking what I see them drinking."

"I can see that."

"Let me tell you a little story," he said.

Jeff took the bottle from his mouth and gave Vick all his attention.

"After I was here for about six months," Vick went on to say, "I meets this fine chick at this market place. I mean she was super fine. We got to be good friends. She invited me to eat dinner at her home. We being good friends, I went. Her pop was cool. He had beer for me. I drank a couple of bottles, got stoned. Momma- san had these pieces of meat she cooked in a pan that didn't look too inviting. Anyway, the three of us sat there, eating this meat and boiled wild rice. Momma-san stayed in the kitchen the whole time we feasted. The meat was tough as leather. I almost thought it was the sole off somebody's shoe."

Jeff interrupted with an outburst of laughter.

"I only had a little piece, even though they tried to get me to eat more. What I ate, I washed down with beer. Afterwards, I left. The next day while we was at the market place, I asked her what kind of meat she had given me, and she told me it was dog meat. She also tried telling me it was the only meat available in his country. G.I.'s and VC killed everything else except for the water buffalo, which is sacred. And believe me. That was the last time I went to anybody's house for anything."

"What about the chick?"

"About two weeks later, the VC, Northern Regulars

passed through her area at night raiding the village, shooting up everything and some of the people. Vietnamese people who knew the both of us told me she was killed, and her parents was taken away."

"Man, that's deep."

"Since I don't know who's who out here, I limit my trust in these people. It's like a 12 hour switch. During the day, they pretend to be your friend. But as soon as the night comes, it's a whole new world around here. You saw the supply building?"

Jeff nodded his head while thinking. "Yeah, some things are starting to come clear. Why do you buy from these people if you can't tell the good ones from the bad ones?"

"Only because I always see them working here."

Some of Vick's friends approached. "What's happening Vick?"

It was the shorter Marine Jeff saw in the hut along with his friend. He eyed Jeff. "You the dude I saw in the hut?"

"Yeah," Jeff responded.

"You trying to get laid already?"

Vick was angered. "Cool it. He's with me. We checking out the sights. You guys must be up to something, or you wouldn't be out here."

"If we are, you'll read about it in the Stars and Stripes. They don't call us number ten for nothin, and that's with a big number ten."

"Number ten means no good," Vick explained. "Keep that in mind."

"I'm learning," Jeff replied.

"Teach him right," the lanky Marine said.

Vick stared at Rich with a burning desire to come right out and question him about the stack of money he gave to Terry, but if he did, Rich and Terry might start bad rumors about Jeff being a rat. It would automatically lead to serious problems. Instead he would try a more settle approach. "Rich," he said in a friendly tone of voice, "I hear your pockets are deep."

Rich seemed calm and collected. "Yeah, a couple of our deals paid off. You interested in borrowing something?"

"No, but I'll keep you in mine."

Rich had a feeling Vick was pumping him for some information that he didn't want to disclose. Rather than get serious with Vick, Rich gave him a pleasant smile with the willingness to move on. "Carry on men. Make sure Jeff sees all there is to see."

The two groups parted. Vick and Jeff went about their way looking around. A gunship swept overhead. Jeff looked up, but he couldn't see much through the fully leafed trees.

They stopped in the shade of and old fully leafed tree. Vick still had wild thoughts of Rich. "Let me tell you something else about those two. "They seem to be some pair. Terry told me he use to be a gang leader in Philly. Rich claims he was a pimp in Chicago."

"I think the both of them are stone crazy," Jeff voluntarily responded.

"Believe me, they are. Both of them like taking things from people. They say it's better to take then to receive. The worse part about them, they don't return things. If he didn't rob Worldley, I can't help but to believe he beat somebody out of some money. Last week Rich was broke."

"I never could understand how people living together can do wrong to a member of their group."

"And Terry, He lies about everything. I think he's just out and out stupid. His famous words are, *I didn't get that from you.*"

"If he gets something from me and start that mess, I'll break his face. That goes for his buddy, too."

"It's best not to get started. Keep your stuff to yourself."

"Solid."

Jeff hears the sound of gunships. He looks up to see it passing low over the market place and continues to travel out of sight.

A short Vietnamese man in black pajamas came running through the marketplace screaming and talking wildly in Vietnamese. He moved down the road, while everyone ignored him. Vick and Jeff watched as they moved along.

Jeff stopped at a table displaying sandals. He lifted a

pair and turned them over. The bottoms were made from used tire tread still in excellent condition. He examined the neat construction.

An elderly woman sitting a short distance away stopped fanning herself. She watched Jeff in silence. "You like to buy?" Came the voice from the quiet woman. "I make very good deal."

Jeff looked up and saw she had black teeth. He was lost for words.

Vick came up behind him and gave the woman a dirty look. "Mama-san, ain't nobody gonna pay ten dollars for a piece of Jeep tire. I'll give you ten dollars for the whole Jeep."

Jeff wanted to laugh but was afraid. She gave Vick a dirty look. "You number Ten, go way."

Vick laughed. The woman got up angrily and charged the table. Vick grabbed Jeff's arm and quickly moved away. The sandals fell from Jeff's hand. One landed on the table, the other bounced off the edge and hit the ground.

A short distance away, Vick released Jeff's arm. "Number ten ain't two words to take lightly in this country. Some of these people are like ragging bulls, especially the older women."

They walked to the outside edge of the marketplace. The man who previously ran out screaming returned with a friend carrying a simple coffin. Jeff watched the two men disappear inside the market area.

"What's with the coffin?" Jeff asked.

"They've got this thing about dying. They bury their dead within six hours in a standing position, or maybe in the same day. I forget exactly how that goes."

Jeff was in deep thought. "What if the person ain't dead, but just has a faint heartbeat?"

Vick wasn't interested. He looked into the area ahead. "You in their territory now. They make the rules. You want to head up to Hill 327?"

"Might as well, how far is it?"

"Not far, we can catch the next truck over there where those guys are standing." He pointed toward the group.

Vick's eyes scanned the roadway for transportation.

They walked to a truck stop. Within minutes, a truck pulled up. The thin trail of dust that followed swept over them as they waited.

They climbed into the bed and Vick immediately took a seat. Jeff was still standing when the truck lurched forward. He lost his balance and almost dove for the bench. "I might get used to a lot of things," he mumbled. "But no way am I going to get used to this." The truck created a screen of dust as it moved toward its next destination.

The market place was just starting to get crowded. Rich and Terry stopped at the soda lady's stand. By now the day's heat had grown. She sat fanning herself with a small hand fan made of straw. Terry leaned over the counter as if to be looking for something. "You want soda," she called out to the pair. Terry straightened up.

"Yeah, we want," Rich, replied calmly. "Give me two. One for me, and one for my partner."

Using both hands, the lady pushes herself from a folding lawn chair. In the process, she crushes one side of her fan, bending it inward. She plays with it for a second or two then laid it on the seat.

"Momma-san," Terry called out, "Hubba, hubba, I'll die of thirst by the time you get around to them sodas."

The lady dug down under the ice and pulled out two sodas and placed them before Rich. Rich and Terry inspect the bottles. She placed an opener on the counter. Terry opened his first and started gulping it down as if his thought was coming true.

Rich looked at Terry like he was crazy. "Give up the opener!" Rich said abruptly.

Terry pretended not to hear him.

Rich grabbed Terry's arm and took the opener from his hand.

Terry took the bottle down. "If you had waited another second, I would of given it to you."

The lady was not amused by their act. "Give me money," she said.

Rich opened his soda, and then laid the opener on the counter. "No problem," said Terry. The pair started to walk away.

The lady became very excited. "Hey," she screamed. "Money, you owe me money." The pair stopped and turned to face her.

"Momma-san, listen!" Rich said.

"I only listen to money."

Rich wanted to make himself perfectly clear to her. He held up both hands. "You asked me if I wanted a soda, right?" The lady looked a little confused, but Rich didn't care. "And I said yeah. You didn't say anything about paying for it."

"I don't care who pay," she said angrily. "Give me money."

Terry dropped his empty bottle to the ground. "I ain't giving you nothing," he blurred out. "I didn't get that from you. I got that soda from Rich. If anybody's gonna grease you palm, Rich is the man."

Her expression had passed the point of total anger. "Oh, nobody pay?" She came from behind the counter. Rich and Terry ran off in different directions. She stopped and raised a closed fist to them. A low mumble could be heard coming from her lips. "I fix you good next time G.I."

The truck traveled at a semi-fast pace. Jeff sat with both arms stretched along the railing enjoying the view. He had never seen rice paddies before. The paddies were built in huge terraces. Water ran through small openings leading from one paddy to the next in an endless stream. Several Vietnamese stood in the water with their pant legs rolled up, doing something to the plants with their hands. In the distance, a unit of soldiers walked along the banks of the paddies in full battle gear, their rifles extended.

As the truck neared Hill 327, the road filled with traffic on both sides, mostly soldiers in military vehicles coming from small side roads. The Post Exchange got its name from the fact that the hill was 327 feet above sea level.

The truck pulled up at the entrance to the PX. All the men jumped out, and Jeff looked around.

The building was huge. It looked to be the size of an airplane hangar. The parking lot was small, consisting mainly of dirt and spotty areas of grass. Vehicles jammed the area. Vick and Jeff got into the short line leading inside. Near the side of the PX, a gunship landed on an asphalt pad. Several men jumped from it and immediately went to the end of the line. They laughed, joked, and horsed around like little kids. Jeff watched for a few moments then turned his attention to several young Vietnamese women hanging around the entrance.

"Are natives allowed to shop in here?" He asked.

Vick noticed the ladies who were well built but small. Their jet-black hair hung straight down their backs. They wore black and white pajama outfits and wide straw hats.

"Only the ones married to military personnel," he said. "Or a friend of a married person who can hook them up."

Jeff watched them as he moved along. The woman smiled at passersby, and he saw how white their teeth were.

A Caucasian soldier walked up to one of the woman, who gave him some money, and then walked off.

"They're probably got something going," Vick said. "That's a fine chick, too. I'd bet he's buying her toothpaste."

"Is she as fine as the one you met in the story you told me?"

Vick smiled at the thought. "Nobody have I seen since her is that fine. She was as fine as the finest silk and as sweet as vantage wine."

Jeff began to laugh. "You crack me up with some of the funniest things you say."

"You got to have some sense of humor around here or you'll go nuts."

They walked inside. Everywhere, there were rows of shelves containing thousands of items. Vick headed toward the record section. Jeff followed but soon lagged behind. *This place has more stuff than some stores back at state side*, he thought. They had reached a point where Vick was almost out of sight. He stepped up his pace in order to catch up.

They walked past the toothpaste aisle, and Jeff saw every imaginable brand. Several soldiers picked up many boxes.

"I see someone's brushing after every meal," he said.

Vick laughed. "They might be getting sweeter kisses. I doubt if they even know how to use a toothbrush, or where to use it other than for rifle cleaning."

They continued walking until reaching the record section. Vick began plucking through the records, and Jeff pretended to be searching for a record, too.

"Did you see that old broad's black teeth back at the market place?" Vick asked.

"Yeah, pretty unsightly."

"Most of the older people's teeth are like that. Before we arrived, the natives chewed this stuff they cut from some special tree, wrapped it in a green leaf, and call the whole shebang, beetle nut. A lot of times you'll see some of these people putting it into their mouth. As a matter of fact, some of them will even roll it and have it hanging out the side of their mouth like a cigar. Whether or not it gets swallow, I never watch long enough." He pulled out an album, flipped it over, and then returned it.

Vick moved to another section and continued looking.

Jeff followed. "It kills the nerve endings during tooth decay to stop pain. But it also turns the teeth black."

"I see God has provided everything a person needs in life."

"I suppose, they should thank him. And the younger ones should be thankful to us." Vick extracted two albums and eyed them. Jeff watched curiously.

Several jets raced low over the building. The loud thrust from the engines echoed within the confinement of the building. Jeff stared momentarily at the sealing. "Man, that sounded like they were coming in here to get us."

"Don't pay them any attention. Most likely they're Marine pilots returning from a air strike. They do that whenever they've had a good day."

"Tell me more about that beetle stuff."

"What about it?"

"Does it get them high?"

"I don't venture out that far. Personally, I've never heard of it firing anybody up. Grass and beer is my limit. Remember those chicks outside?" "Yeah, they sure was looking fine." Them young chicks will do anything to get there hands on a tube of toothpaste." He looked up at Jeff, "except have sex." He shook his finger. "None of that Y stuff. You can only get that if you marry 'em. And I'll tell you that the longer you stay here, the better they'll start to look."

"I ain't quite convinced, only time will tell."

"All of them want to go to the States. They call it the Land of the Big PX." Vick placed the albums under his arm. "That's just what it is too, one big Post Exchange. Anything you want here?"

"No, I can always come back later, if, they don't blow up this place first."

They reached the checkout line. Jeff spotted the soldier, while they were outside, who took the money from the lady, heading in the direction of the toothpaste aisle.

"This place!" Vick commented. "Never. They get more stuff from here than we do. I hope you saw there weren't any patrols or fences around this place."

They went through the line.

CHAPTER FOUR

The temperature outside reached its maximum for the day. Jeff felt grit on his body from sweat and dust. He and Vick walked to the pickup spot, and Vick held the albums over his helmet to ward off the sun's heat.

A helicopter gunship landed in an air-parking zone. Three soldiers dressed in heavy combat gear jumped out and joined the end of the PX line.

A truck arrived directly in front of Jeff and Vick. They, along with several others, climbed aboard. Jeff took a seat quickly this time, remembering the ordeal he went through with the last ride. The truck suddenly jerked forward.

They rolled through the hills and countryside, periodically picking up passengers. After a long, rough journey, they were at the main gate. A military policeman circled the truck, eyed every passenger, and then stood on the driver's step to eye the space on the floor.

Satisfied, he stepped down and waved them through. The gate opened, and the truck moved forward.

Jeff took another look at his new home as the truck rolled along the compound grounds. It resembled a prisoner of war camp. The boundaries had several armed guards patrolling the perimeter, ready to shoot at a moment's notice.

This is as safe as things can get, he thought.

A gunship flew overhead, slowing to land just off the roadway.

The truck stopped at several huts away from Jeff's. Apparently, the truck hadn't been to that area of the base for a while. They would have a little walk on their hands. As the riders prepared to descend from the bed, a fine spray of dust passed over them, adding more grit to Jeff's accumulated layers.

He was exhausted from the heat, the walking, and the rides. He climbed down slowly. Vick was still full of energy and jumped down. "You better start learning how to jump. One of these days the truck's gonna start moving away while you're still hanging on. It's already happened to me. I learned the hard way."

"In time I will. This heat seems to be slowing me down. Where can I shower?"

Vick pointed to a large hut with a canvas top. "We've got water hours. There might still be time."

A young man wrapped in a green towel walked on a pallet boardwalk toward the shower hut.

"It's still running," Vick said. "If for some chance you don't make it, it's open after chow tonight from 7 to 10."

Vick and Jeff started walking down the walkway toward their hut.

"I need one bad. I've got so much dirt and sweat on me,

I squeak with every step. Even my underwear is starting to carry extra baggage."

"This is still your first day. Wait until that becomes mud packs."

Jeff smiled. "I believe I've reached that point."

They walked inside their living quarters. Several soldiers lay on their bunks sleeping. One man sat beside his bed cleaning his rifle barrel. Parts lay on the top of a footlocker, all neatly cleaned.

At lease one man knows how to use a toothbrush, Jeff thought.

The hut was as hot as an oven. No breeze moved inside. The little wall fan still ran, but it wasn't doing much good.

Vick placed his latest purchases into a footlocker under his bed. He lay on the bed and placed his hands behind his head. His helmet rolled off his head. Beads of sweat formed on his forehead.

Jeff prepared for a much-needed shower.

"You doing good so far," said Vick. "I think you might wanna extend your tour."

"Yeah, right. I will if a water buffalo has three legs."

Vick elevated his feet so the heels of his boots rested against the bed railing. His eyes drifted close and his voice became soft as he spoke. "A man's gotta be crazy to wanna stay here longer than he has to under these conditions."

"The guy I was sitting next to at the Processing Center came back thinking this is the greatest place on earth."

"He's one of the crazy ones, I'd bet."

"He is."

The water in the shade of the shower hut was warm, but it felt good, compared to the sweat baths he'd been taking since he arrived. The shower hut was made of wood, stretching three-quarters of the way toward the ceiling. The remaining portion was screened in. The concrete floor had drainage holes throughout. A long string of dim lights crisscrossed the interior. Bulbs were missing from both ends.

Jeff stood under the showerhead letting water run through his hair and down his body. Two familiar voices filtered to him. It seemed the two Marines he met before were entering the hut. They prepared for a shower.

"I don't understand you for the life of me," said the lanky Marine. "You're about the dumbest dude I have ever encountered in my whole life. The dumbest, the dumbest."

Jeff listened as the two men went to their individual showers. He started to recall what Vick had said about them and their schemes. Terry began to lather his face cloth. "Rich," he said. "If I lied, they would've found out by matching the bullets."

Rich let the water spray over him. "Since when has the

U.S. government ever matched a dead animal's bullet with a military person's rifle during war time?"

"The government ain't stupid."

"Are you? Or are you just dumb?"

Rich just happen to look up and saw Jeff. "We meet again."

Jeff stepped away from the shower. "You dudes following me?"

"Terry, did you hear that?"

Terry turned his back to let water run over his head.

"What's your name?" Rich asked.

Jeff hesitated, and then spoke in a deep voice. "Jeff."

"I like a man who knows how to speak up. What do you think about a guy who likes shooting water buffaloes at five hundred bucks a pop?"

Terry stepped out of the shower. "Let it be," he said, angrily. "You ain't got to tell the whole world."

"Sounds personal to me." Jeff packed up his soap, wrapped his towel neatly around his waist, and walked out without giving either of them another look.

Terry returned to the shower. "If you don't stop talkin' about me, I'll punch in your face."

Rich laughed. "Be nice, Terry. Let's not get excited."

"You really got a nerve to be speaking out against me. You ain't no saint."

"I'm sorry Terry, you're right."

Rich started up a roar of laughter, which spilled out into the surrounding area.

"There you go," Terry said with malice, "making fun of me again."

Jeff returned to his hut. Everyone had remained in the same position he left them in. Vick was asleep, and sweat from his head was wetting his pillow. Jeff assumed Vick was more tired than he showed. He decided to let Vick sleep, and then he dressed in clean clothes.

Maybe I'll go sightseeing, he thought.

He walked around the compound. Gunships flew overhead at regular intervals. His eyes followed them until the first set disappeared behind a cloud of puffy gray smoked screen.

This place is well protected, he realized. *If it wasn't for the heat, I'd probably like it here.*

This was Jeff's first permanent duty station. He wished they had sent him to a better location. He read an article in a military paper that stated the average age for servicemen in Viet Nam was nineteen. Perhaps he was meant to be there.

He walked past a barbershop. Sounds of laughter poured through the screen. He hesitated over going inside, then, at the last second, decided against it.

In the far distance, he saw two fighter jets circling an

area and performing an air strike. *Charlie must be acting up*, he thought. *Looks like somebody's having a good time.* From what he saw on television and movies, fighting had no special times for starting or stopping.

He passed a building and saw a basketball court behind it. Two teams raced up and down the court, dribbling, passing, and jumping. Only a small trace of perspiration showed on their clothing.

Jeff went to the seating section and watched the players. The game ended a few minutes later. Several spectators went to join the players for practice shooting. Jeff watched for a few minutes, and then went out to join in.

The ball was passed to him. He bounced it a few times, aimed, and threw. The ball arched up and swished through the net. He got the ball again and made another shot, and then the ball went to another man.

"Let's choose up," someone called out.

Two players set out to select team members. Jeff was asked to play, but, in those few minutes of exertion, he already felt faint from the heat.

"No, that's OK," he said. "It's too, hot."

"If you can't stand the heat," responded the same individual, "stay out of the kitchen."

The remaining player who also failed to be chosen went to the seating area just off the court. Jeff followed, perspiring heavily.

"When does the heat let up?" Jeff asked.

No one spoke or looked in Jeff's direction.

Jeff pulled at his under shirt which was partly sticking to his body. "It feels like 120 degrees now."

"Around October," said a young Marine, sporting a colorful headband.

The game got underway. Skins had the ball in play. One man acting as the team leader brought the ball up court and tried to setup a play. The teams scrambled around the court. The leader passed the ball to an open man who immediately took a shot. The ball bounced off the side of the rim and fell into the hands of the other team. They charged down the court in an organized manner, passing and moving into places until finally, someone took a shot and made it.

Jeff watched in amazement. *Playing in this heat is insane*, he thought.

The game continued with Skins bringing the ball back up court. While the ball was being passed to another member of the team, it was suddenly stolen by a member of the other team and carried back to the basket and deposited. The team leader of the Skins stopped in his tracks. "Something's wrong here. Is there anybody on the bench who can play this game?"

No one on the bench volunteered.

"I don't know how I winded up with the sorriest players

on this base. Come on you guys, I know you can do better than this." He looked to his players. "Let's try it again. This time let me see something. You gotta know how to play or you wouldn't be out here."

The game started up again. One of the Skins dribbled the ball up court while the remaining players took up positions. He passed the ball to the team leader who moved inward and around several players toward the basket, but was finally blocked and came back out to make a weaving jump shot.

"Take control of the ball," he said. "And we'll have ourselves a good game."

The other team started the game going again. They proceeded to move the ball around the court. Jeff left the sports area and walked toward his hut.

A small fleet of gunships flew overhead at low altitude. They landed in a field just behind the mess hall. The sound of engines shifted into a low him. Several gunners leaned forward as they jumped to the ground, quickly moving away from the rotary blades. Jeff looked at his watch and realized it was almost early mess.

Soldiers from various jobs began moving onto the road and walking toward the living areas. Jeff saw everyone wore full combat gear with bulletproof vests. Backpacks weren't required in the compound. He felt odd not wearing any of his gear. From then on, he'd be sure to do so, but, for the rest of the day, he'd wear it occasionally to get acclimated.

He finally returned to his hut, feeling exhausted and drained. To his surprise, most of the residents were back, too. A party was underway. He saw Marines sitting in small groups smoking joints and joking, but didn't recognize any of them from previous transit stations. Then he spotted Vick between two bunks. He was uncovering his new albums.

Jeff walked over to him. The smell of marijuana filled the hut, and a steady stream of smoke rose before Vick from a silver ashtray on his footlocker.

Vick looked up. "Join the party." He placed the album to one side of the bunk, out of the way, and took a half used joint from the ashtray.

"I think I will", Jeff responded. "I could use a lift of spirit."

"At present, it's only a party of one until it grows."

Jeff noticed one of Vick's open marijuana packs near his feet. "You say it grows in the open?"

Vick puffed from his joint. "Sit down." He moved over to make room for Jeff, and then patted a spot on the bed where he wanted Jeff to sit. "You can get away with smoking as long as you don't smoke outside."

"And suppose you get caught?"

"First time, a letter in your folder. Second time, lost of a rank or 15 days in the slammer. Third time, you don't wanna know."

"I would like to."

"Like the baseball empire says."

Vick stood to give an empire's strike call and returned to his seat. He took a few puffs, and then passed the joint to Jeff. Jeff placed it between his lips, but was slow to take a puff.

Vick looked on. Jeff began to inhale gently, and Vick said, "Go head. Take a good puff. It might be the best thing that happened since your arrival."

Jeff took several puffs, and then returned it to Vick. Vick smiled, and placed the joint back on his footlocker.

"You got that right," said Jeff. "It is the best thing that has happened so far." Vick smiled. He placed the joint into the ash tray.

"The greatest thing about this war was its introduction to drugs," Vick said. "Charlie's got the right idea in rolling these babies up and passing them around. This is the good stuff."

Jeff started swaying to the music. "If it's free, I agree."

Vick changed his position to face Jeff. Vick held up the joint and examined it. "I hope the stuff back home is this good. They remind me of the cigarettes called 100's. We call these big boys, Jay's One Hundreds."

"They sure do look awful big. Say, isn't this stuff illegal?"

"Yeah, but who cares? Even the Officers get stoned."

Jeff went into total shock of surprise. "They do!"

Vick moved closer to whisper. "One night when I was walking through Officer's Country, the air was filled with burning weed. I even saw it coming from a hut."

Jeff became angered. "And they got the nerve to be busting people."

"Rank has its privileges."

Jeff felt the effects of the marijuana inside his head. He dismissed the conversation. He wasn't tired any longer, and his perspiration didn't seem to exist. He closed his eyes and patted his leg to the music. He was enjoying himself.

"What do you think?" Vick asked.

Jeff didn't answer, so Vick tried again even louder.

"Great," Jeff finally replied. Suddenly his eyes shot open. "Hold it!" He said abruptly, then walked to his bunk and came back a second later holding one of the packages he picked up on the truck. "Now we can really party." He took his seat again and went back to patting his leg. "The party just grew to a party of two. Hey, that rhymes, grew, two."

Vick laughed. "You are one sick puppy."

"Woo, that is great stuff. I can still feel the rush."

"So what's happening back in the States?" Vick asked.

Jeff slowed his roll with bobbing his head and patting his leg. He gripped the plastic with his teeth and ripped it open. Half of the neatly rolled joints became exposed. "Same old stuff." He removed a joint and handed it to Vick. "I'd give anything to see a real round-eyed chick in a bathing suit just about now."

Vick laughed. "You just got here. It's your first day. You've got a year to go, plus some." Didn't you see enough before you got here?"

"Never enough my good man," replied Jeff.

"I know." Jeff went back to patting his leg in time with the music.

"The best you'll be able to do is dream. Even the Vietnamese women don't own bathing suits. But give or take a couple of weeks and you'll fall in love with some of the lovelier ones."

"I doubt it. There ain't nothing sweeter than a home girl."

"Well, I'll be saying Hi to them for you in less than six weeks." Vick lit another joint and puffed on it, and then he sniffed the stream of smoke. He passed the joint to Jeff.

"I'll save the rest for later," Jeff said. "What happens at night around here?"

"Most of the fellows get high, smoke, drink, and play cards. The stakes are money and Jay's 100. Some of these nuts even dance with each other to the music they play."

His expression changed. "Then there are the rocket attacks, which happen a couple times a week."

Jeff hadn't taken it seriously the first time the rocket attacks was mentioned. But now that his head was clouded with the sweet nectar of marijuana, a sense of fright seemed to come over him. "Twice a week rockets flying around here?" He asked highly surprised.

"The Viet Cong, better known as the VC, are trying to hit this place. I think it's the village people mad at us for not spending enough money with them in this area. They do a little damage occasionally. Most of the time I over look it. But now that I'm getting short, it's starting to play with my mind."

"I don't think I should smoke anymore."

"Them rockets don't stop a party for long. If you don't smoke now, you will later. You'll never make it straight through on being straight and keep your sanity."

"Maybe you're right. It's just that the explosions and gunships got me a little edgy."

"I've been here eleven months. Nobody's been killed yet. We got systems, like night patrols and gunships circling the area at all times of the day and night."

"So, those helicopters I've been seeing flying around here are patrolling this base?"

Vick started to show signs of excitement. "Yeah, they're cool. You should see them in action. They seem to appear straight out of thin air, swooping down on Charlie and boom! Clusters of rockets shooting off. Machine guns firing like mad. You should see Charlie getting up."

"There's always a first time for them to get lucky."

"If they can't hit one of those warehouses, as big as they are, how the heck are they gonna hit one of these huts?"

"Maybe if they didn't smoke opium all the time, they would be more accurate."

"Chow time!" Someone shouted.

Several Marines started preparing to go out. Other Marines joined them.

Jeff stood. "Going to chow?" He asked.

"No. I try to eat as little as possible from there." Vick watched Jeff sway with dizziness. "Boy, you've got a lot to get used to." He laughed. "Maybe you should lay down for a while."

"Maybe I should. That stuff really hit the spot." Jeff walked to his bed and crawled onto the top bunk. It felt good to be motionless. The insides of his head spun around like a top. "I'll go to chow later." He spoke sleepily.

"You won't make it in that condition. Then again, you might enjoy the food better. It's processed from C rations."

Jeff started snoring. Vick stood and looked toward him. "Yep. The man's got a lot to get used to. The man didn't even smoke a whole joint and he's down for the count."

The lights in the hut were bright when Jeff woke. He laid motionless except for his head and eyes. He looked around, but obstacles limited his vision. Loud music filled the air. Unfamiliar voices sang to the music-out of key-and conversations came to him.

He sat up and stretched his arms overhead, twisting his torso as his arms came down to his lap. He needed more sleep and rubbed his eyes with his knuckles. Then he remembered where he was.

"Did you just arrive from the States?" Jeff looked past his dangling legs to see a thin Marine laying on his back in the bottom bunk. He wore green underwear and his dog tags. He stared up at Jeff.

"Yeah", Jeff said. "Something like that."

"I can't wait to get back, I've got two weeks, than I'm out of here."

Jeff straightened. "I've got some time before I can say that. It must be nice to be short. Look like just about everybody's a short timer."

"They tried to empty the base back at State side by sending a bunch of us here all at once."

"Coming in groups sometimes can be fun. I came alone."

"Sometimes I wish I had come alone. I was stationed with these knuckleheads back in the States. I'm stationed here with these same knuckleheads and I will probably go away to another station with these same knuckleheads."

"You got one of those short timer calendars, too?"

"In my foot locker. It's the going thing. Every new day brings a scratch off day."

"I got a long time before I can use those words."

"My name's JM."

"I'm Jeff." He looked toward Vick's bunk, but it was empty. He lay back the bed.

"I must have slept a long time. The sun was high in the sky when I went down for the count."

"It don't take much for the heat to knock you out around here."

"There don't seem to be much by way of temperature change from day to night. It's just plain hot all the time."

"Is mess over?"

JM retrieved his watch from under his pillow. "You've got less than two minutes to get there. It'll take magic to make it in time."

Jeff didn't say anything. JM's voice interrupted his thoughts. "You can always eat at the enlisted men's club. It ain't restaurant style, but it sure beats reconstituted C rations."

Jeff climbed down. "Maybe that might work. I'll try the club and compare. I hope they got real food."

"It's real. Most of the fellows eat there when they have money."

"I don't see how anybody could end up broke over here. There really isn't any place to spend it."

"They gamble it away."

"That figures. Which way is the club?"

"Make a left out the front door. Make a right when you hit the main road. Keep going. You'll see it on the right. It's probably the loudest spot on this base. You can't miss it."

JM rolled onto his side with his back facing Jeff.

CHAPTER FIVE

The club was filled with soldiers. It was a large warehouse converted to an eating and drinking spot. There wasn't anything fancy about it. The walls were bare of signs and graffiti. Low rows of lights, several missing tubes, shone dimly throughout the smoky room. Music blasted out, echoing loudly but barely audible above the noisy crowd.

Two lines moved slowly toward a counter at the far end of the building. Soldiers carried full cases of ten-cent beer cans to tables containing fixed openers. MPs in-groups of two patrolled the area carrying nightsticks.

Vick sat at a table with several friends. The table was stacked with a pyramid of empty cans. Several other cans waited to be consumed.

"I was the arm-wrestling champ back home." Vick bellowed, with his can raised in a salute.

"You couldn't bend a string in half," a medium-built soldier replied.

Vick bent forward, almost falling against the pyramid, but he managed to grab the table's side and stopped himself. He placed his entire arm on the table and raked it sideways, bringing down the pyramid. Cans flew in all directions.

This time Vick set his elbow near the table's center. "Come on, pecker head", he shouted angrily. "I'll show you which way the wind blows. I may not be able to bend a string, but I sure can break your knuckles on this here table."

Two MPs rushed to the scene, their nightsticks in hand. One of them walked around to stand beside Vick. "Do I detect some kind of a problem over here?"

"We're cool." Vick said, staring at the MP's .45 in its holster. The sound of the two men tapping their sticks against their hands made him calm down. "For real, we cool. We got this. Just a slight accident with the cans."

"Clean up this mess," one MP said. "We'll be back."

"Just give us a couple of minutes. We got this. As soon as I handle this little matter, we'll stack' em back up, I promise."

"Do that. You got 10 minutes."

"Anything you say." Vick was starting to become upset again.

"Who wants to be the first to get his knuckles cracked?"

Vick got on one knee, and the MPs walked off.

One of Vick's friends, just finishing a can, held his face close to Vick's. He tried to keep the conversation between the both of them by whispering. "Quit while you're ahead," he said. "You're drunk."

This made him furious. "You think so?" He shouted. "First I can't bend a string and now I'm drunk. Come on! Try me!" He banged his other fist on the table, and the remaining cans jumped. "Scared? You scared pecker head?" His blue eyes were glassy.

"We'll see who's the pecker head," the husky man responded. "You asking for it."

The soldier passed his unfinished can to the Marine besides him, and then he set one knee on the floor, ignoring the beer staining the cloth, he learned forward to make his height equal to Vick's and raised his arm.

They locked hands. Vick's face tightened as he made a quick jerk. The locked hands lay at a forty-five-degree angle in his favor.

Vick smiled. His opponent smoothly brought their arms back up, his expression neutral.

"You think I'm easy or something?" The Marine asked.

"I like competition." Vick gritted his teeth and inched the man's arm down to halfway, then the man fought back.

Vick's knuckles crashed to the table, and everyone burst into laughter. He laid his head on top of the table in the midst of spilled beer.

Jeff entered the club, passing two MPs near the entrance. The sudden noise made it hard to think. He stood momentarily, surveying the area. Then saw a snack bar to one side of the lines waiting for beer. An overhead sign listed items for sale.

He strolled casually toward the counter.

"What'll you have?" The man behind the counter asked as he wiped his hands on his apron, waiting to serve.

Jeff glanced at the overhead menu. When Jeff didn't speak, the man said, "I don't know why everybody stares at that menu. It's been the same since this joint opened and I doubt if it's ever going to change. I'll come back after you decide."

He began walking away.

"No," Jeff said quickly. He stared at the man. "I want to order." Then turned his attention toward a section of the menu. A state of silence set in between to two of them.

"It don't take a rocket scientist to make a decision about this menu. What you gonna have?"

Jeff brought his eyes down to rest on the counterman. Then back to the menu.

"I'll have one of those steaks." He pointed toward the menu. "The one with onions and a little catsup, and a large soda-any kind."

The man started writing up the order. Sounds of fallen cans gave Jeff just cause to quickly face the crowd but because the seating area was as so large, he was unable to identify the location where the noise came. His head moved side ways, then froze when he saw Vick shuffling cards in his hands. Jeff looked back for the counter man and didn't see him.

I'll give him time to prepare the food. He walked toward

Vick, who was looking down at his cards and talking. "We would stay up all night drinking beer and playing basketball." He looked up upon seeing two legs standing next to him. His face seemed to glow with a smile. "Heat knocked you out, I see."

Jeff could barely hear him. "I just needed a few winks."

A Marine carried an opened, full case of beer to the table. Everyone took a can except Jeff. He glanced back at the snack counter and saw the man coming out with his meal. "Gotta get my grub from the snack bar." He left and returned a few minutes later only to find the case of beer empty. Jeff laughed. "Does everyone here drink like fish?"

One of the men belched loudly. "Gotta refuel for tomorrow's heat wave. Can't be caught dry. If you don't want to dehydrate, you better get with the program."

"I'm not a real beer head. I'll try sticking with water."

"I said the same thing when I first arrived. Now I drink at least one six pack a day."

A fight broke out several tables away. MPs rushed in, and the area surrounding the fight broke out in cheers. Vick's group drank without looking up, but Jeff stood to watch the action.

"See one fight, you've seen 'em all," Vick said. "Let's go. We've got a card game soon. I want a seat this time."

Everyone else stood and started moving away from the

table except Jeff who climbed up on a chair to get a better view of the action.

Vick looked back at Jeff, who was still watching the fight. "You coming?"

"Yeah, hold tight." He hadn't heard Vick clearly.

Vick went back to tugged his leg. "Let's beat it. In the future, you'll see better ones. Come here around 11 p.m. You'll see a real fight. That's when the club closes."

Jeff jumped down, picked up his food and drink, and hurried to catch up with the others.

"On to the game!" Vick said.

They walked around the fight spectators who threw cans at the combatants and the MPs.

There was no moon overhead, only a few lone stars. Jeff trailed behind the group, eating and drinking as they moved along. He gazed up into the sky. What caught his attention were the many streams of tracers flying through the air not too far away. They seemed to appear from some magical point in midair, arch down, and disappear. In the same area, explosions set off brilliant flashes of light and echoing booms through the night's heat wave.

A small group of gunships raced at low altitude across the compound, heading toward the flashing lights. For the first time since he arrived, Jeff felt really frightened but afraid to show it. It came from the combination of fighting in the distance, darkness over an unknown land, and the possibility of an aerial attacked. He realized he was in a war.

The group ahead showed no sign of discomfort. *Maybe after I've been here a while,* he thought, *this will seem like just another day.*

Another group of gunships raced overhead. The men looked up at them, and all their side doors were open. Jeff was barely able to see the gunner manning his .50 caliber machine gun. Small, deadly rockets sat in fixed position on the sides of the gunships. The group moved to one side of the road to let a jeep pass.

"I bet those gunners don't get much sleep," Jeff said to no one in particular.

Vick glanced at the gunships. "They're Marines. Tough. The best. Love action."

"Cut the bull," someone called out. "The supply men are the best."

The whole group screamed out, displaying a raised clenched fist, "We are the best."

Jeff watched until the airships were small dots in the night sky.

Rich and Terry sat on vacant footlockers in the hut, leaning on Terry's lower bunk. Both faced each other. Rich shuffled a deck of cards, then dealt five to Terry.

"O.K.," Rich said. "Be cool. Don't give yourself away."

Terry picked up the cards, trying to act professional. "These feel like new." He squeezed them with his thumb and fingers.

"Never mind that," Rich whispered. "You learn how to read these, and our money problems are all over. We can clean up around here."

Two Marines came into the hut. Rich watched them in silence. They walked into the back as Terry stared at the cards.

"How do you read them?" He asked.

"Not so loud!" Rich whispered. "I don't want the whole world to know what's going on."

"O.K.," Terry whispered back.

"In every corner, there's a circle divided into twelve parts with another circle in the middle. Look for a dot in there somewhere."

Terry brought the card closer to his face. "It's in the eleventh space."

"Right on, Brother. That's a Jack." Rich seemed a little disturbed by the way Terry held the cards. "Don't hold the cards close to your face. We can't let them know what's going on."

Terry became confused. "Jack of what?"

"You don't need to know what kind of Jack it is. Don't be so stupid. All you need to know is if you can win the pot."

"Oh, O.K." Terry moved the cards close to the table.

Rich just look at Terry and shook his head in denial. Terry placed the five cards back on top of the deck. He divided them in half, placing the top half on the bottom, and then held the deck slightly close to his face again. Rich placed his head between his hands. "Terry, I just said, not to hold them up. Do you want me to talk in Vietnamese?"

"No, I wasn't thinking." Terry lowered the cards.

"Try another card."

Terry looked in silence. When he found it, a smile appeared on his face. "It's in the center."

"That's a king. The twelfth dot is a queen. The first one's an ace, and the rest are regular numbers. Check 'em out for a while. I'll go see about the players."

Terry looked up at Rich all surprised. "There ain't much to this. I've already got it."

Rich tried not to sound angry. "Go over them anyway, practice. Make sure you've got it down pat." And DON'T move the cards close to your face."

"I got to give you credit. You are smarter than you look." Rich stared at Terry for a moment, while shaking his head from side to side then walked out the front door.

CHAPTER SIX

Rich, Vick and his group arrived at the gambling hut together.

"This must be the place." Rich said, as he held the door until everyone else walked in. Then it occurred to him. "Rich, being polite doesn't always get you a seat. It didn't the last time."

Jeff saw Sam and JM already sitting at a table. The interior of the hut was decorated like a recreation room. Only a handful of soldiers were present. Two faced a dartboard at ten paces. One dart was embedded in the center circle, and two others were just outside it. Another dart was being thrown. Beside that area was an unused dartboard. Tables were set up around the room for games.

They went to the table where Sam and JM sat. All the checkers were removed, but the board was still there, printed on the tabletop. A few players strolled around the room, picking up abandoned chairs and bringing them to the table.

Jeff watched as the group sat at the table. The well-lit area made the gold border of the checkerboard flicker.

Vick released a long belch. "There goes the foam from that last six pack." He wiped his mouth with the back of his hand. "I feel good," he bellowed. "I'm ready. What's the game?"

No one spoke.

"Jeff, you in?"

Some of the men looked at him as Vick took a worn deck of cards from his back pocket.

"No, I'll watch," Jeff, said calmly. "I'm not a real card player."

JM remembered Jeff had to eat at the enlisted men's club because he missed chow. "It cost money to eat at the club. Win a few good hands and you could be eating like a king all week."

"The food was better at the club, so I found out," Jeff said, casually." Maybe I'll get Vick to teach me a couple of games."

"Good old Vick," Sam said. "Vick the card shark been doing most of his dining at the mess hall. I wonder why."

"Hey!" Vick was quick to respond. "Don't play me cheap. I can afford to eat anywhere I choose. I just prefer to spend most of my money at the beer line."

Another player slapped his hand on the table. Jeff jumped. The noise caught him by surprise. The player was growing impatient. "If your talk was as good as your card playing, you'd be rich. Let's get this game rolling for whatever it's going to be."

Jeff walked around the room until he found a chair. Part

of the back had been broken away. He took it to an area near the gamblers, and parked himself where he would get a good view of the game.

"Let's play acey duecy," Rich said. "That way, everyone can get into the game at once. I like big pots."

Vick set down the cards and put his hands in his lap. "Fine with me."

Everyone else agreed.

"Let's draw cards to see who deals." JM pulled the cards a little closer to himself and set down the deck. Everyone eyed the deck in silence.

Stretching his finger like tentacles, JM squeezed the deck to form a perfect stack. With the same hand, he lifted half the deck and took the top card from those that remained.

He kept it face down and replaced the cards he held in his hands. He took a peep, smiled, and then nodded to the others. Everyone else drew, keeping his chosen card face down.

This was Jeff's first time watching a card game. He saw the players' orderly mannerisms as they played. If the game interested him, he'd join later.

JM turned over his card and showed a king of diamonds. One by one, each player turned his card over except Rich. So far, no one had beaten JM. Rich lit a cigarette and everyone waited.

"Come on," Vick said. "You're holding up the game."

The others agreed. Rich took the cigarette from his mouth and placed his other hand over the card. "I'm a gambler. Let's see how much heart you got." He set down his cigarette and removed a dark-brown wallet from his back pocket. "I'll give you a chance to make a few bucks before the real gambling begins."

With the one hand, he removed a ten-dollar bill, laid it flat on the table, and then pushed it toward the center of the table. "Match this if you think I can't beat that king."

"You ain't drunk," Sam said. "So you must be crazy." He took several bills from his pocket. "I've got five toward that bet."

Vick seemed impressed. "Good man."

Sam counted bills from one hand to the other. "Okay gambler. You so sure of yourself. I got ten more to ride with this."

Now Rich was staring at Sam. "Like I said, I'm a gambler. It's only money. I'll cover that, too."

Sam placed three five's on the table and slowly pushed them up against the ten. Rich took another ten and pushed it into the pile. Three other men produced enough money to cover the bet. Rich lifted his hand, and his card remained face down on the table.

"Looks like the betting is heating up before the game starts," said JM. He reached for Rich's card and then held it out for everyone to see.

"Easy money," Sam said. JM turned it over and everyone saw an ace of clubs.

"Easy money." Rich raked in the pot. Jeff stood and stared in amazement.

Was it a trick? Jeff wondered. *Or is he just good?*

Rich separated the money as he laid it out before him. No one else seemed surprised.

"Let's start the game." Vick was eager to play. "I got money to burn."

Rich picked up the cards just as a jet zoomed overhead at low altitude. A single burst of machine gun fire rattled off. Everyone was quiet for a few seconds. JM stared at the door momentarily, then returned his attention to the gang. "Man, I'm waiting for the day when I can go somewhere in peace and not have to think about running for cover."

"This ain't no different then where I'm from," Rich said. "We got old cars backfiring all the time and gun fire everyday on the streets."

"Well," another player said. "Over here we got these crazy broads from the market place with plenty of our money. Do you think Charlie's trying to bring some of them to this game?"

"I think so," Sam answered. "I always thought Rich liked those women with the black teeth. He's always going to the market place to see them."

Everyone broke out in a burst of laughter. A joke session seemed to have started up.

"I like them all," Rich stated. "I don't care if they are blind, cripple or crazy. And from 25 to 55, fast speed to slow speed. If they can't walk, I'll carry them."

Everyone continued to laugh except Jeff, who felt a sense of embarrassment for the natives. He had been taught to give respect to everyone regardless of their physical condition or situation. Meanwhile, Rich shuffled the deck and fanned them across the table for everyone to see. "These babies are old and worn. I bought some new ones a little while ago."

"It would be nice to use a new deck," said Vick.

Sam held his hands up face high trying to imitate Vick. "It would be nice to use a new deck. You sound like my sister."

Vick didn't like that remark. His face dried up. "I didn't know your sister was a man," he shot back.

The group let out a oooH!

Sam realized he had struck a sore spot with Vick. "Okay, you got over this time."

The room became quiet. "Maybe my luck will change," Rich said. "Give me a minute. I'll run to the hut and grab 'em."

JM rubbed his hands together in wonderment. "If your luck gets any better, we'll be eating from the mess hall and drinking water from a tanker." A sense of humor could be felt returning to the group. Rich moved back. "Not a bad idea. Maybe you guys need to clean your system out of all that E.M. Club's food before hitting the States." He walked off at a quick pace out the front door.

"How'd he do that?" Jeff asked.

JM picked up the cards and examined the backs carefully. After a few seconds, he threw them down. "Luck."

CHAPTER SEVEN

Rich hurried to the hut. The sound of distant artillery fire, people talking, records playing, and insects calling made the night seem alive. Terry was still playing with the cards when Rich entered. He went quickly to him.

"Ready?" Rich asked.

"Yeah," Terry smiled as he looked up to Rich. "I've got it down pat. Wanna test me?"

Rich was in a hurry to get back. "No. Let's go. I ain't got time. I'm dealing. If we fool around too long, they might wanna pass the deal off."

Rich walked away. Terry took his time moving from the footlocker. He picked up the deck and shuffled them as he went down the aisle. Rich waited impatiently outside. Finally, Terry came out. "Terry, you slowing down on me. You got to move quicker than that. Come on. Let's hurry."

"What you in such a big hurry for? Chill! It ain't like we going to a fire. It's only a game. You can always get the deal."

Rich walks off at a quick pace than stops to face Terry. Terry seems to be logging farther behind while still shuffling the cards, but stops shuffling when he sees Rich looking back at him.

Rich waves his hand for Terry to speed up, but Terry stops walking.

"It's money, Terry," he said, trying to stress its importance. "Money you could use to pay me back for that stupid buffalo you wasted. Don't just stand there, let-us-go."

"Oh! We working together on this deal and I ain't getting nothing?"

"I didn't mean it that way."

Terry looked confused and mad. "Just exactly what did you mean?"

Rich was starting to get angry because of the wasted time, but he knew he had to convince Terry to participate. "I'll give you a little less than half, and you won't owe not a thing. We cool with this deal?"

Terry had to think for a moment. "We cool." He knew payday was still a week away and the gang did have five hundred dollars between them. He would come out on the better end of the stick.

They started walking briskly toward the hut. Rich saw Terry was shuffling the cards. Rich placed his hands over them.

"What's the problem," Terry asked.

"Stop! You'll burn off their faces and make the backs fuzzy."

"They feel good. I'm trying to break them in."

Rich stared him down. Terry stopped and held the deck by his side.

Several low flashes went off in the far distance, followed by their faint explosions.

"How many times are you gonna tell me. You trying to find away to call me, you know what?"

"What are you talking about?"

"I might be about an ounce slow, but I'm not stupid."

"Okay. I promise not to disrespect you anymore if you help me pull this off. You won't ever hear me again call you stupid or dumb."

"It's about time."

"Listen good, now. When we get there, sit across from me."

"Why not next to you?"

"It don't work like that, now listen. Off and on, watch for my signal. It's important that we make this work."

"What kind of signal?"

"You'll know when the time comes." Terry looked at him, and Rich pointed to Terry in a mean fashion. "I know how you are. Don't mess up. If you do, you'll be sporting your body bag cause I ain't backing you up."

"You mean we partner and you ain't got my back?"

"Hell, no. These guys are serious about those dead Presidents. That's why I gave you time to practice."

"Come on." Terry stepped up his pace. He saw Rich was

starting to lag behind. "Come on, I got this. No problem. You'll see."

Rich started to catch up. "I hope so. We got everything riding on this move."

When they walked in, Sam said. "It's about time you got back. I was starting to think you went to get mama-san."

"Had to wait for Terry," Rich said, coldly. "You gotta warm him up to get him moving. Momma-san probably has twice his speed."

Some of the group laughed under their breath. Rich wasn't amused. Terry placed the cards on the table. Several explosions went off in the far distance. Everyone became still and silent momentarily. Rich took his seat and pointed to where Terry should sit. "Terry, grab a seat. Your money spends as good as ours." Terry took a chair from another table and returned, sitting it between JM and another man. The area was tight. He squeezed it partly into the small space.

JM became very upset. "I was here first. You ain't like me. They call me JM because I'm like a Jungle Man. I'll get all over you like something fierce. Now sneak off to another spot."

Terry showed no emotions. "What does all that talk got to do with me sitting here?"

"You crowding me, and I don't like it."

"So you saying you gonna go ape, and do something to me because you, Jungle Man?"

Rich gently waved his hand before him. He was calm. "Let him sit there. After a few hands, he'll be broke and out of here."

JM glared at Rich.

"Go ahead," Rich said. "Be nice. He's not disrespecting you."

JM stared at Terry, but Terry ignored him and passed the deck to Rich. Jeff moved a little farther from the table, not knowing what to expect next. JM moved slightly to let Terry in. Terry moved his chair up close to the table. Vick adjusted his position and folded his arms. "When you guys finish playing musical chairs, I'm ready. Let's get it on. I feel hot."

"And so it is, you old drunk," Rich said. "Ante up one good ol' Georgie Porgie."

Vick rubbed his hands together. "I'm gonna be the luckiest drunk person you ever saw."

Everyone placed a dollar on the table, and Rich smiled as he shuffled the cards. They watched him carefully.

"Don't burn off the faces," said Terry.

Rich suddenly stopped, eyed him, and then shuffled once more. "Here we go. Every man for himself, win, lose or draw."

Several hands were dealt. Two players won a little, but most lost.

The pot grew until it held several bills of singles, fives, and tens. Jeff continued to watch, and noticed Terry was constantly watching Rich. The more he watched Terry, the more intrigued he became. It seemed Terry wasn't paying much attention to the game.

Suddenly, Jeff remembered the warning give to him by Vick that Rich and Terry were con artist. He focused on both men.

It was JM's turn to bet. He sat one place ahead of Terry. Rich dealt him two cards face up. JM stared at the ace of spades and six of diamonds.

"That's a good hand if you ask me," said Rich.

"I'm not asking you," JM replied. He was deep in thought.

JM took two tens from his small stack of money and placed them along side the cards with his fingers resting on the bills. He raised his eyes to meet Rich's who was staring him down.

"You playing with scared money, Jungle Man?" Rich asked.

"No. Sixes and aces isn't my cup of tea."

"If I had your hand, I'd bet the pot."

JM looked nervous. "You aren't betting. I got this."

"Sorry Mister tough Jungle Man."

They watched JM, and then he raised his fingers to let the money fall from his damp fingertips. "I'll bet the whole twenty."

"Are you sure?"

Vick became uneasy. "You heard him. Turn over the top card!"

Rich slammed a card down over JM's pair. It was a four of clubs. JM looked a little disappointed. Rich raked the two tens into the pot. "You're a better man than me. I just knew you had a winner."

JM didn't reply.

The room went silent. Terry received the next cards - a queen of hearts and five of spades. Rich held the deck out at an angle so he could read the backs better.

Jeff noticed Rich's foot reaching out to tap Terry's under the table. Terry looked at the pot, then at Rich.

"How much is there?" Terry asked.

Vick counted the pot while everyone watched except Terry, Rich, and Jeff. Terry looked into Rich's eyes, and Rich nodded the go for it signal. Jeff moved slightly closer to observe what was about to go down. He had seen the signal, but didn't know what it meant.

"Eighty-eight dollars." Vick returned the money to the table's center.

Terry stared at the pot in hesitation. "A queen and a five,

eighty-eight dollars." He shook his head in denial. "I don't know."

Rich looked down at the cards in his hand once again. He gritted his teeth in frustration about Terry fooling around so long to make his move. It became hard for him to avoid looking at Terry. He looked at the men throwing darts. "Scared money travels in packs. You and JM been hangin' around together?"

Terry was quick to respond. "And what is that suppose to mean?"

Vick started to wonder what was going on between them two. *If Rich had to give money to Terry to pay his fine, then where did Terry get money to get in the game.* He decided to throw a curve ball into the conversation and maybe get lucky. "Speaking of scared money, by any chance, that money might be Worldley's?"

Terry was taken by surprise. His eyes grew larger.

Rich was quick to respond. "Terry, play your hand. Don't pay any attention to him."

Vick wasn't going to let the conversation die. "Rich, I hear you been passing out money. Terry, did you get your share?"

Terry was afraid to speak. He kept his eyes on his cards.

Rich was determined to get Vick off their backs. This was not the place for this type of conversation, but he would meet Vick head on. "What's up with you?"

"Worldley told me he was robbed just before he left."

"If you looking for trouble, I'm just the man who can handle it."

The remaining gamblers was taking all this in. Jeff got a little nervous thinking a fight between the two of them would break out at any moment.

"Rich didn't rob nobody." Terry surprised everyone when he opened his mouth. "I was with him when he found it".

"I bet," said Vick. "In his foot locker?"

Rich was getting a little edgy. "I ain't gonna feed into this. I found the money. Nobody asked around about it, and I didn't hold it out for grabs. If Worldley can't hold onto his money, that's his problem."

Sam had heard enough. "Worldley ain't here. You guys can fight over that mess later. I'm here to play. Let's get back to the game."

"Yeah," said another player. "I need money to buy beer for tomorrow."

Terry stood, went through his front pockets, pulling out some bills and displayed them on the table. He sat down again and counted out eighty-eight dollars. "That's a lot of beer money gone to waste if I lose."

"Don't worry," someone whispered. "This group won't let you dehydrate." Terry took one last final look at Rich, but Rich had everyone looking at him and was in no position to confirm their win. Terry pretended to be betting on gut feelings. "Let 'er rip," he bellowed, trying not to smile as he pushed the money forward.

Rich tossed him the next card with a small slap. It was a ten of clubs. Terry's face lit up as he raked in the pot. Everyone watched in disbelief that Terry had cleared out the whole pot.

"Darn!" Sam said. "There goes the pot."

Terry started sorting the bills before him. "I got enough here to take a beer bath. If I win another pot like this one, I'm gonna buy everybody one." He held up one finger. "One beer. I hope everybody can get a taste."

"Very generous of you to treat us," JM said.

Jeff couldn't believe he just watched two con artists at work. Out of anxiety, his hand shot high over his head.

Vick looked at him, his face expressionless. "What's up?"

Jeff tried to speak. His lips moved, but no words came out.

"You okay?"

He nodded yes, then lowered his hand, and Vick returned his attention to the game. "Everybody ante up again," he said.

Jeff bit on his bottom lip and then said, "good play." He didn't want to be accused of starting a fight, nor did he want to be blamed if someone was hurt or killed. The truth would only be known between him and the con artists.

Rich collected the cards and shuffled. "This game is based on luck. It's my turn to win."

"No, I'm winning this time," Vick said.

Jeff couldn't watch any longer. While the next hand was being dealt, he walked out into the night air.

CHAPTER EIGHT

The sound of artillery fire was louder. Jeff stood before the gambling hut and watched bursts of light fill the sky. There was almost twice the amount of activity as before. Jets whistled past in the distance.

What have I gotten myself into? He wondered. *There's a war going on all around the camp, and soldiers inside fighting each other. Friends cheat friends. The other people do drugs.*

He looked through the screen at the gamblers. Rich and Terry were having a good time, while working on another trick. Jeff walked toward his hut.

Music blasted from inside as he neared the door. A threesome stood outside, drinking from a bottle. A small cigarette was passed to the last drinker. He inhaled from it and coughed hard enough to start gagging. The other two laughed.

When Jeff came near the smoker's, the one coughing held out the joint blindly for him to take, but he refused with the wave of his hand and walked into the hut. The smell of marijuana gripped his nostrils. He said nothing as he walked to his bunk. One Marine in the back said something funny, and the group around him laughed.

Jeff sat on his bed in silence, staring toward the front

door. Suddenly, the squeaking door was pulled open. A tall, but thin Marine came in and made his way down the aisle toward Jeff. He stopped at Jeff's bed when he noticed Jeff staring at him. "I thought I recognized you, "Jeff said. "But apparently I was mistaken."

"No harm done. I have been mistaken for a lot of people. So, how's it going new guy?"

"Long hot day."

"I know what you mean. I've been here two months and I still haven't adjusted."

Jeff extended his hand to the Marine and they shook hands. "Finally," Jeff said." I ran into somebody who's not short."

"There are plenty of us around. You probably been looking in all the wrong places. Did you meet some of the guys in the back?"

"No. I've been with Vick most of the day."

"Come on back."

"No. I got plenty of time later."

"Suit yourself."

"Well, tomorrow will be my first day at work. No doubt I'll run into a few. You live in this hut?"

"No, just passing through, looking for a friend. I couldn't stay here. The smoke gets so thick at times, you can cut it with a knife."

"You smoke?"

"Not really, but every now and then I'll catch a few blows with the fellows."

Jeff was surprised to hear that. "All this free smoke and you ain't really down with it?"

The Marine felt good about himself. He sort of puffed his chest up. "My health is most important to me. It's bad enough being here. I want my mind straight and my body as strong as possibly. Look, I gotta go. See you around the base."

"Yeah, good talking with you."

The Marine continued on his way. Jeff laid his head on the pillow and stared at the ceiling. The world around him had taken on a new dimension. Suddenly, he jumped to the floor and pulled his footlocker from underneath. After removing a writing pad and a pen, he pushed it back into its previous position and hopped back on his bunk to write. To make himself feel more at eased, he laid to one side, propping himself up with one arm. He jotted down a few words. Shook his head in denial, and then ripped the paper from its pad. Now, his thoughts were starting to come clear. He wanted to let someone know just how he felt. His mom was the most understanding person he knew, *good old mom*. He would write to her.

Dear Mom,

I never thought, in my wildest dreams, just after my nineteenth birthday I'd wind up someplace having the same characteristics of hell. I'm glad to say that after one day here, I've seen people, places, and things that make me feel proud to say 'I'm an American'.

My military friends have been kind to me today because I'm new around here. Given time, they will probably treat me just as unfavorably as they treat each other. I can live with that, I'm also a Marine.

An old friend of mine, Vick, took me on a safe tour to see the natives. Some were kind, others, I had my doubts about.

I have yet to experience war, see death, or feel the vibration of destruction. I hope I don't, but being that I'm stationed in a warring country, and attached to a supply unit, it's inevitable. I'm starting to understand the meaning of the word poor. These people don't have things we take for granted - even basic things like running water, electricity, or even a house. I have yet to see any child under the age of five wearing shoes or fully clothed.

He stared into space, thinking about the next line. A loud burst of rifle fire interrupted his thoughts.

All conversations in the hut died. The only sound came from various cassette and record players. Those were quickly silenced. He moved up into a sitting position.

Suddenly, bursts of machine gun fire mixed with the rifle fire, then a clicking sound echoed through the air as if it was coming gradually nearer. Jeff heard men running outside. He looked outward through the small screen area into the night, barely seeing soldiers with and without combat gear. They ran wildly from huts to in-ground bunkers. Something began to tell him things weren't right. He started to feel worried.

The clicking grew louder, and other clicking sounds were added. The first set sounded as if they were directly over the compound. Someone from outside started screaming. "In coming!"

Everyone inside the hut grabbed his war gear. Jeff watched with intensity. Seconds later, three explosions rocked the area simultaneously. By now, they were moving fast. Some, partly clothed, raced in file a long with the fully clothed ones outside through the front and back doors. More clicking sounds blended with rifle and machine gun fire.

Now, Jeff really became terrified. No one had instructed him on what he should do in this type of situation. He jumped down to the floor, pulling his writing gear with him. Instincts about safety became automatic. He pushed the footlockers out from under the bottom bunk, and then proceeded to crawl underneath.

The last Marine running toward the door saw part of Jeff moving along the floor, in a prone position, stopped and grabbed his arm. "Get out of here!" He yelled. "You want to die?"

The Marine yanked Jeff to his feet and held him as Jeff was pulled down the aisle. Rockets zoomed overhead. Jeff was pulled out the door so fast they almost broke it off it's hinges.

Another barrage of rockets exploded several huts away. Debris filled the sky. The Marine and Jeff raced toward the nearest bunker.

A jet zoomed overhead at low altitude, firing a burst of fixed-wing rockets. The flashing lights illuminated the area long enough for Jeff to see the bunker they were headed toward. He ran so fast, he almost knocked down the Marine ahead of him.

It was dark inside. Without light, Jeff moved as far as he could to a wall. When he couldn't go any farther, he knelt and tried to make himself small. The noise from the ground fire, jets, and the gunships made Fourth of July fireworks sound like a water balloon fight.

The only light came in through the single door. Gunships

roared overhead, firing .50-caliber machine guns. Jeff began to recite the Lord's Prayer.

"Our Father who are in heaven...."

Suddenly, everything stopped except for a few sounds of rifle fire. Jeff stopped praying. From his crouched position, he saw the outline of someone inside the bunker moving toward the entrance and outside.

Silence gripped the area. Jeff slowly calmed down.

"All clear!" someone shouted from outside the bunker.

"That was close," a voice said in the dark.

"You said that last time," another voice responded.

"Well, it's true. This was the closest sound of destruction I have ever heard in this hut area."

"You bugging out. The longer you stay here, the worse you get."

"Hey, man. I've got ten days left. If I could see my watch, I'd tell you how many hours too, before I get on that plane. I Pray to God I don't have to go through another night of this."

"You should be an old pro with these games."

"Let me tell you something. I had so much time to do when I first arrived that I could care less about living or dying, but as time passed, I've gotten to be a short timer, and now that I've lived through this hell or nightmare, and the end is in sight, I want to live to be free again".

"And I thought you was all gung-ho".

"There ain't no glory in death. I still remember the three things told to me when I first arrived at the Processing Center. My choice right now is the airplane ticket."

"That's my choice too. I ain't gettin wasted for nobody. Let's check out the damage report."

The men stood and walked out the door.

Jeff sat with his back against the wall. "Jeff," he said softly. "You really did it this time. You left three squares, a roof over your head, and a pleasant environment to come here where Charlie doesn't like you. Your food comes from a can dated three to five years ago, and your house is on the verge of destruction. I know why Vick called this place, Unpleasant Pastures. I gotta stop talking to myself. I'm the one bugging out."

The smell of mildew in the bunker reached his nostrils. It was damp inside.

He went out into the night air. Soldiers ran toward the recreation hut, which was lost in a thick, high blaze.

Vick! He thought. Jeff ran toward the burning structure. By the time he arrived, a ring of soldiers stood around the blazing building. He made his way to the front of the crowd by easing a soldier to one side. The soldier gave him a hard look, and then continued to watch the blaze.

The back half of the hut appeared to have taken a direct hit. Pieces of it lay everywhere. "Charlie finally invaded our living quarters," the soldier said.

A fire truck arrived, but there was no siren going to warn of its approach. People moved aside to let it through. Jeff looked into the blazing destruction. Off to one side, a bucket brigade worked hard trying to reduce the flames.

"Yeah," said Jeff, "Charlie done what no man thought was possible." Thinking Vick might had left the hut, Jeff searched thought the packed crowd in hopes of locating him.

"It's a darn shame," Someone said as Jeff passed by him. "They were such an odd but good bunch of men."

Jeff turned to look at the soldier. "Did you know who was inside?"

The soldier looked into Jeff's eyes. Jeff felt the sudden rise of fear as the man looked briefly at him, then back toward the blaze.

"I'm looking for an old friend, Vick."

The man kept his eyes focus on the structure. "If he was in there, he'll be going home early. They took several bodies from here to over there." The Marine took his eyes away long enough to point to an area off to one side of the burning structure.

Jeff made his way to the rear of the crowd and rushed to where the Marine had directed him. Several bodies lay in line, covered with sheet. An MP stood, guarding the bodies.

"Looking for someone in particular?" Asked the MP.

"Yes," he said softly. "A good friend of mine named Vick."

The MP stared at him. "You know you're not allowed near the bodies?"

"I know. I just wanted to see for myself. If it's him, I...I wanted to thank him for being a friend."

The MP didn't move. After a moment, Jeff turned to go.

"Come here."

Jeff stopped and turned. The MP waved him forward, and then he bent and lifted the sheet off the first one. Jeff's heart raced as he looked at Sam, JM, and Terry's bodies.

Then he saw Vick, his face covered in several bloody cuts. Jeff knelt slowly beside him.

"Don't touch anything," said the MP.

Jeff didn't move. Tears ran down his cheeks.

A commotion started to grow louder among the sightseers as the crowd grew. And a convoy of Helicopter gunships moved overhead in slow formation, heading toward the area from which the rockets came.

ABOUT THE AUTHOR

Charles Feggans was born in Philadelphia, June 7, 1943 during World War II. At the age of six, he and his mother moved to Trenton, New Jersey where he has claimed home ever since. After graduating from High School, he joined the United States Marines Corps. Ten years he spent as a baker. Dissatisfied with his direction in life, he returned to Trenton. Since then he has graduated from Mercer County Community College and Thomas Edison State College, both in New Jersey. This is his first novel. *Unpleasant pastures* is an inspiring journey. He plans to continue writing stories about real life people.

What inspired the author to write about his subject comes from visual observation during his tour in Vietnam during the war. He has felt the heat, seen the destruction from rockets, and lived in fear just as the people within the story while stationed at a camp.

Printed in the United States
By Bookmasters